The Lady Loves a Scandal

Christina McKnight

ISBN-13: 978-1-945089-39-8

La Loma Elite Publishing

PRAISE FOR CHRISTINA MCKNIGHT'S NOVELS

THE THIEF STEALS HER EARL

"When I started reading this book I could not put it down...it caused another book-hangover for me. I wanted to see how things would go when the truth of Judith came out and how Simon was going to handle it...loved it."-*Sissy's Book Review*

"Jude and Cart's story is such a delight! So refreshing to see the hero shy, socially awkward and not super wealthy. I love it...This was definitely one of the best books I've read this summer." -*Reviews from a Thrifty Mom*

FORGOTTEN NO MORE

"This author has made me love historical romance again." -*TwinsieTalk Book Reviews*

HIDDEN NO MORE

"The storyline was really good, the writing was great. So smooth and engaging, I was able to zip right through the story, it flowed so well. I love finding new to me authors and with this wonderfully written story by Ms. McKnight I've found a new historical romance author."-*Bound by Books*

CHRISTMAS EVER MORE

"*Christmas Ever More* was a wonderfully written festive novella full of hope, renewal, love, and new beginnings. If you're a fan of Christina's Lady Forsaken series, this is a must. Even if you aren't caught up, this stands well enough on its own to be a lovely addition to your holiday reading list."-*Literal Addiction*

BOOKS BY CHRISTINA MCKNIGHT

The Undaunted Debutantes Series
The Disappearance of Lady Edith
The Misfortune of Lady Lucianna
The Misadventures of Lady Ophelia

Lady Archer's Creed Series
Theodora
Georgina
Adeline
Josephine

Craven House Series
The Thief Steals Her Earl
The Mistress Enchants Her Marquis
The Madame Catches Her Duke
The Gambler Wagers Her Baron

A Lady Forsaken Series
Shunned No More
Forgotten No More
Scorned Ever More
Christmas Ever More
Hidden No More

Standalone Titles
The Siege of Lady Aloria, a de Wolfe Pack Novella
A Kiss at Christmastide
For the Love of a Widow
Earl of St. Seville
The Lady Loves a Scandal
Bound by the Christmastide Moon
Bedded Under the Christmastide Moon

DEDICATION

To my readers,
Never let a little scandal dull your shine!

ACKNOWLEDGMENTS

A huge thank you to my fellow authors; Erica Monroe, Ava Stone, Amanda Mariel, Dawn Brower, and Deb Marlowe. Together we created an amazing anthology—and I couldn't dream of a better group of women to call friends.

There are so many people who support my passion for writing. Here are a few I am blessed to call friend: Marc McGuire, Lauren Stewart, Erica Monroe, Amanda Mariel, Debbie Haston, Angie Stanton, Theresa Baer, Ava Stone, Roxanne Stellmacher, Laura Cummings, Dawn Borbon, Suzi Parker, Jennifer Vella, Brandi Johnson, and Latisha Kahn. Thank you all for accepting me for, well, me.

A very special thank you to my editor, Chelle Olson with Literally Addicted to Detail, your skill and professionalism surpass all that I expected. Chelle Olson can be contracted by email at literallyaddictedtodetail@yahoo.com.

And to my proofreader, Anja, thank you for embarking on yet another journey with me.

Cover design and wraparound cover design credit to Sweet 'N Spicy Designs.

Finally, thank you for supporting indie authors.

PROLOGUE

After nearly a year of courtship, I, Lady X, am fairly confident in announcing the betrothal of one Viscount Galway of Barrow Burn, Northumberland to Lady Sybil Anson, most recently of London, by way of Paris, France and sister to the newly entitled Eighth Earl of Lichfield. As you, my dear readers, may remember, Lady Sybil is new to town after spending her childhood in the city of love. This author can do naught but imagine the draw between the stoic, reserved Lord Galway, and the young, impish foreigner, Lady Sybil. I am certain all of society will agree, both Lady Sybil and Lord Galway come with sordid pasts.

~ LADY X, 10 February 1815

London, England
February 1815

LADY SYBIL ANSON crouched ever lower until her rounded bottom nearly touched the rough, wooden slats of the floor of the hackney, her elbow resting precariously near a grease-covered metal piece. The constant jostle of the ramshackle conveyance as it moved leisurely through the crowded London streets was enough to loosen the pins securing her long tresses and sent shooting pains up her back to her neck. Certainly, a proper lady of the *ton* would never have used extreme trickery on her maid, fled her home under cover of night, traversed the dangerous alleys of London until she reached a well-traveled area of Regent Street, and hailed the first hack she spotted…all while keeping her hood pulled low, and the hem of her gown pulled high off the filth littering the streets.

Though no one claiming even a speck of good sense would ever describe Lady Sybil as *proper*.

Peculiar, maybe.

Entrusted with an odd sense of humor, commonly.

A lover of scandal, certainly.

However, it wasn't that she was any more unusual than other debutantes, or in possession of a dryer wit than many men of her acquaintance. The main difference was that she saw no need to mask her true self.

Cast the blame on her upbringing in France; her finicky, absentminded mother; or the fact that her older brother raised her. Whatever the reason, Sybil stood silently by as others used her past as fodder during her first Season.

Little did any of them know that Lady Sybil Anson did not give a bloody fig about their staunchly held beliefs on the ways a proper English miss should conduct herself while in polite company.

The hack turned a sharp corner, sending her sprawling to the far side, her wrist and knee slamming against the high, wooden rail.

"Damnation and hellfire," she muttered. She flexed her fingers and rotated her wrist to test the damage.

Pushing back to her seat, Sybil was encouraged to see they'd finally entered Grosvenor Square, where the roads were not riddled with potholes, and the evening traffic was sparse. Unfortunately, with the affluent neighborhood also came increased illumination from the row of townhouses flanking her on both sides of the street. Before departing her home, Sybil had made certain her hood shielded her from view and hid her long, dark hair. Even the sleeves of her cloak hung past her fingertips, the hem likewise long.

The guise was not to stay above scandalous gossip.

It was not her name—or that of her brothers—she worried over.

Blessedly, the hack slowed and turned once more, this time into a well-manicured circular drive, shadowed from above by the looming stone edifice of the Galway Townhouse.

"Stop here, sir," Sybil called. The command earned her a questioning glance from the driver. "I have no plans to draw you into any unsavory dealings, I promise you."

She knew the townhouse before her very well. Far better than any unwed lady should know a lord's London home. If anyone were to ask, she'd deny ever stepping foot into Galway Townhouse without her aunt or another relation as her chaperone.

That Lady Sybil proclaimed herself in love with Gideon Lyndon, Viscount Galway, meant little to the gossips about London. That she was certain he held a tender for her as well was also of little import—at least until the betrothal contracts were signed.

It made little sense that her being outside Gideon's home after dusk with no chaperone would be taken as proof of her ruined status and have scandalous repercussions on her family's already tarnished name. But in less than a day's time, after the contracts were duly signed and witnessed, a minor indiscretion between betrothed couples could be overlooked. And people thought her peculiar.

It made Sybil miss her time in Paris all the more. Days and nights spent free from worry over societal ridicule. People, young women included, given the opportunity to explore themselves and the city without fear of scandal. There were still rules to be followed, of course, but nothing as crushing and oppressive as her British counterparts.

She shook her head at the thought. No, not her British counterparts. Her country, her home, her future.

"Ye get'n down, miss?" the driver hissed in a hushed whisper. "I got me other fares ta earn."

"I need you to wait for me." Sybil smoothed her cloak over her gown, made certain her hood was high, and checked the driveway for onlookers—it was abandoned, at least for the moment. "I will not be overlong—" At the driver's hesitant stare, she continued. "And I shall pay triple your usual rate."

She'd known the man would agree long before he nodded in concurrence.

Another lesson she'd learned during her time in London.

With the right amount of funding, anything was possible—the finest gowns by the most sought-after modistes, the agreement of kept secrets, the quashing of gossip, and London hackney drivers willing to pick up and deliver any passenger without question.

It likely also helped that her brother was the Earl of Lichfield and wed to the daughter of a wealthy marquess, eccentric as her new sister-in-law may be.

"Lovely." Sybil stood, pulling her sleeves down to cover her gloves as she took hold of the side of the conveyance and swung her leg over the rail, finding the large wheel with her foot before bringing her other leg over to join the first as she hopped to the cobbled drive. Clapping her hands together to remove any dirt, Sybil turned a bright smile on the driver. "Thank you, sir."

His birdlike eyes widened, and he appeared almost impressed by her resourcefulness.

Sybil's mother referred to her daughter's practicality in all matters as *gumption*.

Another thing lacking in every London debutante

she'd met—and even some men.

Another carriage rattled down the street behind her as the wind increased, pulling at her hood and the hem of her cloak. The moist, earthy aroma on the breeze foretold the coming rain, which was likely to fall sometime during the early morning hours and reduce to a light drizzle by first light.

Sybil wrapped her arms around her midsection, determined to be safely home and abed before the first drops assaulted the filthy London streets. She made her way along the hedge to a shadowed area at the side of Lord Galway's townhouse. The small, cobblestoned space was blocked from view—neither a passing coach nor the butler at the front door would spy them. Even if someone knew they were present, the darkened alcove masked them entirely.

The racing of her heartbeat at moments like these was fairly addicting.

The risk, the intrigue, the barely contained need that boiled inside her...

Sybil sped up as she moved down the hedge, arriving at the spot where she'd told Gideon to meet her. A part of her feared this excitement would fade once they were officially betrothed—not to mention once the wedding took place. Certainly, their adventure would continue even when they no longer had to sneak about town to see one another without a proper chaperone.

Holding her breath, she waited, certain she'd hear the familiar, solid footsteps that were Gideon's trademark. He was confident, though never arrogant. He was kind, yet never with an air of pity. He was stoic, but Sybil knew the man beneath the dour, reserved facade.

The minutes passed, and a spike of anxiety coursed through her. Had Oliver, the bookseller, gotten her message to Gideon in time? Was the viscount in residence this evening, or had he gone to his club, never knowing she wished to meet?

A tendril of doubt wormed its way into her thoughts.

Doubt. A funny emotion—and one that never pertained to Lord Galway.

He was dependable to a fault, unlike so many other things in Sybil's life.

She released a heavy sigh when, finally, his heavy footfalls sounded on the cobbled drive, moving in her direction.

"Sybil?" his deep baritone was almost disapproving and menacing in the darkness. "It is after midnight. What are you doing gallivanting about the dangerous city? I thought Mr. Oliver quite mad when he delivered your note earlier."

Her heart, only moments before racing with anticipation, almost stopped when Gideon stepped into the shadows with her, throwing his arms wide to greet her. Without thought, she rushed into his waiting embrace.

"I had to see you, Gideon," Sybil gushed, perturbed by the weakness evident in her voice.

"I will be round tomorrow—or, I suppose, later today—to sign the contracts."

"Are you certain?" Even after their yearlong courtship, Sybil feared Gideon would change his mind. Cry off...leave her.

"Of course," Gideon said, his words clipped, but he pulled her closer still and tucked her head under his chin. "The negotiations are complete. Everything is finalized except our signatures on the paperwork. I am to arrive on the morrow at eleven sharp. I anticipate that everything will be official by noon."

"Silas has forbidden me to join you until it is time to put my name to the agreements."

"It is the way of things, my love." Her heart skipped a beat at the endearment, but she pulled back from his embrace, and he rubbed his hands up and down her arms as if he could impart a bit of warmth. "Business is handled by men, though that does not mean I value your input any less."

"I think you appreciate more than my input, my lord," Sybil said coyly.

"I value much about you, my lady."

"Like what?" She couldn't help but provoke him. It was in these private moments that Gideon allowed his usual stoic exterior to crumble and fall—at least for a few moments. "Tell me, or I shall remain here all night."

"Your complex musings," he said with a smile, leaning forward and placing a kiss on her forehead. Sybil couldn't halt her giggle. "Your enchanting brown eyes."

"My mud puddle murky eyes, you mean?" It was their game, and Sybil allowed her lids to slide shut. Gideon placed a kiss on each.

"Your button nose that is usually stuck somewhere it does not belong," he mumbled before pressing his lips to the tip of said appendage. "And your rosebud-red lips."

When he didn't immediately kiss her, Sybil opened her eyes and gazed up into his light gray stare.

Heat pooled at the junction of her thighs.

Part of her hated that Gideon could bring her so quickly to desire while he remained seemingly unaffected.

"You are a poet, my lord," she whispered.

"And you are the enchantress who feeds all my poetic ramblings," he countered.

"I love you, Gideon Lyndon," she confessed, pushing to her tiptoes until their lips were a mere inch apart. "I cannot wait until the day I am Viscountess Galway."

"Would you love me as much if I were a..." He paused, pursing his lips in thought. "A fishmonger? Or a vendor in Hyde Park or at Covent Gardens?"

"Would you risk your reputation as a gentleman to meet me in a darkened drive if I were an orange seller outside the theatre?"

"Yes," they both chimed in unison.

"Let us hope we never test those fates." Sybil laughed.

His reserved veneer returned as his eyes searched hers. Sybil was uncertain what he hoped to find.

"It was highly improper and unsafe for you to journey out tonight," he scolded. "What if something had happened? Or worse yet, you were taken and disappeared?"

Sybil grinned up at him. "Come now, Gideon, for all the talk of London's perilous streets, I know not of a single person being taken—especially the sister of an earl, the soon-to-be betrothed lady of a viscount."

His eyes darkened as he stepped back from her, his head shaking.

"We have met in similar ways the entirety of our courtship," she chided. "I am still whole."

Sybil patted her chest to prove she was unscathed, yet her attempt at dispelling his unease did naught to return them to their previous light banter.

"We have convened in a shielded grove in Hyde Park, at the bookseller off Bond, and outside both our homes, but never, ever so close to the witching hour." He pressed his lips to hers, but it was not their usual sweet kiss. His lips were firm and almost punishing. "If anything ever happened to you, I would not be able to go on."

He held her stare until she consented, "I will do nothing so foolish again."

His lips softened, and the hint of a smile returned. "Although, I can admit having you at my home—at least, *outside* my home—at such an hour, brings many scandalous thoughts to mind."

"Oh, do tell—"

A horse whinnied close by, and Sybil glanced over her shoulder to see the mare tied to the hack as it stepped from foot to foot and tossed its head back with another neigh.

"I should go," Sybil said.

"I will accompany you home." Gideon glanced toward his townhouse. "Allow me to summon my carriage."

Placing her gloved hand on his arm, Sybil called for him to wait. "Your coach could be seen, and that would lead to scandal. What if someone saw? I promised I would not bring any disgrace upon you."

"I cannot, in good conscience, allow you to—"

"I made it here without incident, my lord," she rushed to say.

"Be that as it may—"

The deafening sound of horses' hooves pierced the air, sending the hack's mare into another bout of distress as a lone man on horseback raced into Gideon's drive. The rider pulled to a halt mere feet from the front door, and Sybil feared for a moment that he was set on riding right through the wooden portal.

Gideon stiffened before her.

"Are you expecting someone?" Sybil asked.

Had her brothers discovered her missing? Had her maid returned to Sybil's chambers to check on her mistress, found her not in residence, and alerted the entire household?

Sybil sighed in relief when the man dismounted and stepped into the pool of light cast by the torches hung outside Gideon's door.

"Wait here," Gideon demanded, but he did not await her reply as he stalked from the shadows and addressed the rider, stopping him before the man pounded his clenched fist on the door.

The men stood close as they talked in hushed whispers that were carried away on the night breeze before they reached Sybil.

Finally, Gideon nodded and motioned for the man to go inside as he turned and started back toward Sybil.

Halting before her Gideon asked, "Are you certain

you will be safe to return home alone?"

Suddenly, Sybil wasn't sure at all, but she would risk the unimaginable to avoid admitting that she'd been wrong to depart her home at midnight for their final clandestine meeting before their betrothal was officially announced.

Not trusting her voice to remain steady, Sybil bobbed her chin up and down.

"Good," he sighed. "I will see you on the morrow. Dream joyfully in your slumber."

"Who is the man?" she dared ask. "He seemed rather urgent in his arrival."

"It is nothing to worry about," Gideon said, but it did little to ease her apprehension. "Only a long-standing matter I've been attempting to rectify for some time."

Sybil's brow pulled low. If Gideon had hidden something from her before she hadn't noticed. But she was not foolish enough to think that a man arriving during the middle of the night was of no consequence. Questioning Gideon further would gain her nothing, however, unless she wished to start their betrothal with the mark of a nagging woman.

Gideon pulled her into his arms as his finger traced down her cheek and along her jawline. A shiver raced the length of her spine, and she pressed her body against his.

Soon enough, they'd be free to touch, caress, and kiss one another to their hearts' content, but for now, Sybil needed to return home before anyone noticed her missing. Besides, Gideon obviously had other matters to attend to before meeting with Sybil's brother in the morning.

"Farewell, my love."

"Until later." Sybil grinned up at him, determined not to allow the man waiting inside the Galway Townhouse to ruin this moment for her.

Rising to her tiptoes again, Gideon's lips met hers

in the dark, and their mouths moved in a rhythmic rightness that always seemed present when she and the viscount were together.

It was rather advantageous she'd fallen in love with a man her family not only approved of, but whom society also held in high regard; although, even if Gideon were the son of a tailor, Sybil would love him still.

He broke away from her. "Now, hurry home."

With a final laugh and smile for her soon-to-be betrothed, Sybil turned and ran to the waiting hack, climbing back up without any assistance.

"Hanover Square, please," she called after taking her seat. She would do all in her power to remain safe—and that meant risking being sighted when the driver deposited her before her brother's townhouse. "Dering Street."

As they pulled away from Gideon's drive, she glanced over her shoulder. A groom had come from the stables and was nodding vigorously in response to whatever the viscount said.

Something was amiss. Sybil was certain of it, even if Gideon thought her concerns were eased.

"Pull over here," she called, her voice rising above the clop of the mare's hooves and the creaking of the hack wheels. When the driver did not immediately heed her command, she yelled. "Stop. Here. Please. Stop now."

Relenting, the driver pulled up on the reins.

Sybil turned to face Gideon's drive, the neighboring properties now blocking his house from view.

"Miss," the driver said, not bothering to hide his irritation. "It be late."

"Do shush." Sybil held her finger to her lips. "Only a few more moments, I promise."

If the late-night visitor had only come about a business matter, he would leave in quick order, allowing

Gideon to find his bed. The seconds ticked by, turning into minutes as the night wind howled down the street, trapped between the rows of townhouses on both sides.

The driver passed the reins from hand to hand, and the resounding jingle was nearly masked by the wind.

Sybil kept her eyes trained on the drive a few houses back.

Finally, the sound of hooves rang out once more on the cobbled ground as not one but two horses raced from Gideon's driveway and headed in the opposite direction of her stalled carriage.

One was the lone horseman from before, but the other...

Sybil's breath stuck in her throat, her lungs burning as she attempted to swallow.

The ebony horse accompanying the other rider was Goliath, Lord Galway's prized stallion.

She was helpless to do aught but watch the pair ride off into the night.

CHAPTER 1

My fair readers! It is with abundant relief that I am the first to inform you of the latest on dit. Spread the news far and wide, I beg of you. Viscount Galway has returned—alive, unscathed, and unwed. If you will remember, Lord Galway was all but betrothed to Lady Sybil Anson when he mysteriously disappeared. Alas, he has returned. Though I dare say he will now be called upon to answer my questions, be he a thief, pirate, in financial ruin, or simply a runaway bridegroom. This author awaits the viscount's reasons for abandoning the fair Lady Sybil in such a deplorable manner.

~ LADY X, 20 March 1816

London, England
March 1816

GIDEON, VISCOUNT GALWAY, slipped through the crowd in the entrance, handing his coat to a manservant before using a group of matrons with atrocious headgear as a shield to enter the Lichfield ballroom—and by the Graces above, avoiding the receiving line. This included the Lord and Lady in residence. The evening was proving uncomfortable enough as it was without coming face-to-face with Lichfield. Gideon's breeches were too tight, and his cravat had been tied so elaborately that his chin had no other choice but to tilt up an inch, making it necessary to stare down his nose at every person he passed as he skirted the fringes of the room.

He hadn't been required to adhere to London fashion for over a year. Nearly fourteen months outfitted in sack breeches and tunic shirts the likes of which were guaranteed to gain no notice from those around him, yet were vital to survival at sea or dodging men who hunted him as he traveled through rural Scotland and England. He needed, above all, to remain invisible while in plain sight. He'd allowed his hair and facial stubble to grow for months until he no longer recognized his own countenance when he happened by a looking glass.

How were the bounty hunters to locate Gideon if he could not spot himself?

Constricting breeches, fresh, white linen shirt, and precisely executed cravat—all the fancy trimmings of a proper lord. In all his time away from London, Gideon never had time to miss such formal attire.

And now he found it highly bothersome.

Peculiarly, he was no longer the highly revered and respected Viscount Galway, but the itinerant stumblebum who kept to the shadows by the docks, who asked outlandish questions at the alehouses, and the nomad known to stow away on any ship leaving port.

Shouts of good cheer and celebration sounded behind Gideon, causing him to flinch and duck his head before the action restricted his breathing. He must keep moving. No one gave him any notice as he searched the room. Easily, he spotted Lord and Lady Lichfield as they departed the receiving line and accepted flutes of sherry from a passing servant. Wisely, he kept in the direction that had him moving opposite of his host and hostess.

Rumors of Lady Lichfield's talents for clairvoyance, while not known about London, had been spoken of in hushed whispers between he and Lord Lichfield's younger sister.

He was not yet prepared to make his return known to Sybil's elder brother—nor his wife.

First, Gideon needed to speak with Sybil.

Bloody hell, at this point, he'd be satisfied to lay eyes upon her across a damned ballroom. He'd suffered every day—no, every *hour*—he was separated from her. His heart had broken when he rode away from London with Giles, bound for the port in Edinburgh...their destination unknown at that point. It was still a fog of painful memories even now.

Gideon reminded himself that he'd had no choice.

Nor had his promise to Sybil come with the expectation of breaking his pledge.

He'd loved Lady Sybil from the moment they met over two years before.

He still loved her with everything within him.

Yet, he couldn't neglect his responsibilities. The promises he'd made long before they fell in love and pledged to spend their futures together.

This night would give Gideon the assurance that the words spoken all those months ago still held true. That even after all this time—through their separation, and his disappearance—Sybil's love for him had not changed.

One fact remained: his affection for Sybil had not waned. Not in the least bit. In fact, it had only grown stronger with time and distance. No matter the oceans that separated them, regardless of the land between them, despite the silence Gideon had lived in for the last year...he loved Sybil.

With time to explain, at least what he could at this

juncture, Gideon was certain Sybil would understand and forgive his absence.

There was no other outcome Gideon could foresee.

A passing couple strolled by, the gentleman leaning in to whisper something to the finely dressed lady on his arm before their eyes narrowed on him. Averting his gaze, Gideon continued past the pair, risking a glance over his shoulder to see that both had turned to stare in his wake.

He'd heard the rumors. Giles and Charles had all but crowed with mirth at the outlandish tidbits reported by Lady X on her gossip sheet. It was one of the rare things that brought a sense of normalcy to the trio—an indulgent, insipid, haughty woman's senseless ramblings in London's gossip rags—as they moved about the land, avoiding the men who hunted them. According to Lady X, Gideon had been a pirate, a highwayman, in debtor's prison, and even living with a Cheapside actress during his year of absence.

It was preposterous, insulting, and so far from any truth that Gideon couldn't help but admire Lady X's ability to keep society's attention away from the actual matter at hand.

There were days—and long, frigid nights—where Gideon would have given anything to be back in London, even in the dangerous area of Cheapside.

Gideon stepped back until his shoulder blades pressed into the ballroom wall and he searched the milling crowd for her familiar, dark brown tresses—not ebony like the rest of her family's. He listened for her light laughter—not the deep, gruff chuckle of her siblings. He kept his other senses tuned to her scent: lemon and a fresh, country breeze—not the perfumed acidic aroma that most of London preferred.

Lady Sybil Anson was here, and Gideon would find her.

Finally, her familiar crown of cocoa locks came

into view, and his heart swelled, his chest tightening until he thought no breath would pass his lips again until he stood before her, his arms around her, and Gideon was confident that she was safe.

Lady Sybil spoke with a matronly lady, the elder woman's chin bobbing up and down as she seemingly agreed with whatever Sybil was saying, affording Gideon a clear profile view of Sybil's enchanting smile. If the woman's head moved any more erratically, her hat—complete with plumage and feathers—would be thrown to the floor and trampled.

As if Sybil sensed she was being watched, her lips pressed together into a firm line, ending her conversation with the matron. The elder woman took her cue and moved on, leaving Sybil alone as her eyes grazed the ballroom. She didn't spot Gideon immediately. No, the moments passed with agonizing slowness until Sybil's brown eyes met Gideon's gray stare.

Her back stiffened, and her glare narrowed on him before the lovely pink in her cheeks drained—leaving her pale and almost sickly looking.

Anyone who noted her stark white complexion would have assumed that Lady Sybil had seen a ghost.

In many ways, that was true.

As the seconds passed, her questioning expression turned to surprise as the grim set of her mouth changed to a startled *O* and her eyes widened. Just as quickly, the shock left her, and her entire body hardened. Anger flared in her eyes, and the muscles bracketing her mouth tensed.

She was utterly captivating...and Gideon could not fathom how the music and dancing continued around them, groups and pairs moving about the room, oblivious to Sybil and him, not a single person affected by the wonder that was the woman Gideon loved.

Soon, they would gain someone's attention, and word would spread of Gideon's arrival in town. He couldn't stop the gossip, but he needed a few more days before all of London became abuzz with the news.

Unease settled like a rock in the pit of his stomach when Sybil's arms crossed over her chest, no doubt wrinkling the expensive silk of her bodice. Her cheeks flamed scarlet.

She had every right to be angry—furious, really—with him. He'd disappeared on the eve before their betrothal contracts were to be signed and had left nothing but a vague note. He hadn't reached out to her since he left London. He could tell himself he did so to keep her safe, to avoid jeopardizing her well-being, and to give the men hunting him no reason to turn their focus on her, but Gideon had badgered himself every day for not finding a way to return to her sooner.

And he wasn't safe yet. Charles was still considered a deserter. And Gideon was responsible for abducting the man from the British Navy ship setting sail for the new world. There were bounty hunters searching for both of them, and he'd rather perish than have them discover his connection to Lady Sybil.

Gideon cocked his head toward the terrace doors, but Sybil shook her head in refusal. His chest fell, and his exhaustion nearly overtook him. She didn't want to see him, wished not to speak with him. He'd risked coming to the Lichfield townhouse for nothing.

Blessedly, she tilted her head and indicated a door nearly hidden from sight by a tall, robust palm. When he nodded curtly, she turned and moved toward the exit. She hadn't said no to his unvoiced request to speak with her, Gideon realized. This was her home, and she knew the precise places for them to talk privately…which wasn't the crowded terrace.

Gideon was helpless to watch her—the sway of her hips, the bounce of her hair as it trailed down her back, and the way a man stepped into her path, halting her progress.

Gideon's entire body tensed, and he stalled himself

from moving directly through the throng of dancers to Sybil's side, slipping her arm through his, and guiding her from the room...and away from the lord blocking her exit.

Splotches of color invaded his vision as he allowed the anger to thunder inside him.

It was the only place he would allow his fury to show itself.

He'd been away from London for over a year with no explanation. Many thought him dead—or at least never to return. Why would Sybil not also listen to the gossip about town? Blaming her for his actions was unthinkable. She was an innocent in everything.

Even now, Gideon knew that his reasons for seeking her out were selfish.

Sybil patted the man's arm, nodded, and continued on toward the door.

And just as quickly, Gideon forgot about the lord—the way he'd leaned in toward Sybil during their brief conversation, the way he'd smiled down at her, and the familiarity of Sybil's fingers upon the lord's sleeve.

Instead, he pivoted, spotting another door, nearly invisible, about five paces away.

Gideon had wished for this day, dreamed of this very moment for over a year.

Soon, Sybil would be back in his arms, and all would be right again.

Sure, Charles was still a hunted man. And Gideon would continue to be responsible for stealing an impressed man from a British Navy ship—the bounty looming over both their heads not going away anytime soon.

But Gideon would have Sybil once more. She would know he loved her and hadn't forsaken her. Yet, he feared that her heart had strayed, and that Sybil could no longer pledge her entire self to him.

CHAPTER 2

It appears that Viscount Galway has cried off, leaving Lady Sybil unattached once more. One can only assume the viscount saw the error of his ways with connecting his family, and good name, to a young woman of dubious upbringing.

~ LADY X, 22 February 1815

SYBIL'S BODY QUIVERED, threatening to collapse beneath her at the mere thought of Gideon…back in London. Alive. Unharmed. Whole. Tangible. Things she'd begged, pleaded, and prayed for all these months.

Glancing over her shoulder, she made certain the Duke of Garwood wasn't trailing her as she slipped from the ballroom into the darkened corridor. The hallway was on the far side of the house, nowhere near the retiring rooms or the foyer, meaning she and Gideon would be afforded the necessary privacy for their talk—for her to berate him properly. That was after she ran her hands up and down his arms, trailed her fingers along his jaw, and pressed her body against his—all to confirm that her eyes were not deceiving her.

He was real, and he was in her family's townhouse.

Pain shot from her hands and up her arms as her nails bit through the thin silk of her gloves and into her palms. Sybil halted, taking a deep breath, but the air stuck in her lungs, refusing to leave.

Gideon, the Viscount Galway, had returned.

It had been over a year. Countless nights spent crying herself to sleep until her brother, Silas, threatened to send her back to France to live with their mother. Endless months of gossip at her expense. And Gideon thought he could just waltz into her family's home—during Sybil's sister-in-law's birthday celebration, no less—and catch her gaze from across the room?

When her stare met his, Sybil's heart had seized in her chest, the room had turned scalding hot, and, as the seconds ticked by without the image of him evaporating like a mirage in the African desert, a soul-deep chill had settled upon her. Sybil wanted to allow the elation of seeing him to overtake her, surround her, and insolate her. She wanted nothing more than to beat a hasty path through the room and throw herself into his arms. Her need to touch him, speak to him, and smell him was so strong, she'd nearly thrown caution to the wind and run to Gideon, the London gossips, scandal, and the past be damned.

Everything and everyone could go to the bloody devil.

Only Gideon mattered.

And he was safe. He had returned to her.

But then the duke had chosen that moment to step into her path, cutting off her escape.

The Duke of Garwood. Odd that His Grace had set about courting Sybil over the previous Christmastide season, yet she still did not know the man's given name, nor was she overly concerned with deepening their attachment. Certainly, he was a most dashing man. A wealthy, connected lord. A proper businessman whose staid manner extended into his courtship of Sybil. There were no late-night rendezvous outside his townhouse, no stolen kisses in his opera box, no inviting banter that left Sybil shivering with pent-up passion and lust. Her stomach had never fluttered at the sight of him, nor had her knees threatened to give way when they were close.

But the duke was available and willing, and they'd all but announced their plans to become betrothed.

With Gideon gone, Sybil hadn't cared overmuch whom she wed, or if she ever did for that matter.

The duke had been easy enough to sidestep in the ballroom.

But not as easily forgotten here in the abandoned hallway.

The thought only increased her irritation at Gideon—and his foolish timing.

Damnation. Until a few moments ago, she'd convinced herself that he was dead, for what other reason could there be for his absence? For him staying away from her so long.

Sybil had been a fool. She'd pined for Gideon all this time. Had written countless letters, sending them anywhere she thought he could possibly be: his townhouse, his manor home by the Scottish border. She'd been so desperate, so broken, so crestfallen she'd even enquired at the London residence of the Galway solicitor. No responses ever came from his homes, and his solicitor had claimed ignorance. He stated he hadn't heard from the viscount either. Yet, no one came forward to claim Gideon's title. The process of proving her love deceased hadn't been brought before the courts.

That only left one unmistakable fact: Sybil was indeed a fool.

And Gideon was to blame for it all—her heartbreak, the gossip and scandal, and even Sybil's courtship with Garwood.

Footsteps sounded on the polished floor as someone with a long, heavy stride rounded a corner and moved toward her in the darkness. The hair prickled on the back of her neck. This was her home, and never had she been overcome with a sense of peril while in it. It could be anyone traversing the halls during the ball—a servant, a guest, or even a criminal bent on thievery.

"Sybil."

Her pulse hammered, her blood rushing through her veins. It was the exact thing she'd longed to hear since the night she watched Gideon ride away: her name uttered in a breathless whisper crossing his lips. She could almost feel his breath cascading across her neck as he called to her again.

"Sybil."

Belatedly, she realized he'd called her because, just as she could not see him in the darkened hall, she was also invisible to him.

"Lord Galway." Her clipped tone halted his movement. How long had it been since she'd spoken to him in such a formal way? He'd bid her to address him as Gideon since their second meeting, at least when they were afforded a spot of privacy. "What are you doing here?"

"I—"

"Where have you been? Why did you leave London? What reason did you have for not showing to sign the betrothal contracts?" Each question was punctuated by the stomping of her foot, which made little sound due to her soft slippers. Slamming her heel into the floor should have released a bit of her fury, yet only her words echoed in the cavernous hall. "The only explanation that suits is that you found yourself dead and unable to keep your promise. However, here you stand…over a *year* later. Can I assume you were gravely injured and unable to send word to me?"

He exhaled, the sound barely audible where he continued to stand in the shadows. She wanted to bid him come closer, yet, she did not trust that she would suppress the urge to close the distance between them.

"I sent a note," he whispered.

"Saying you would return as quickly as possible." An image of the missive, nestled in her stationery desk, came to mind. The scant, simple words. "Do you think your return has been quick, my lord?"

He stepped closer, and Sybil was shocked to realize he'd only been a few feet away. "I returned as soon as it was safe to do so."

"Safe?" She receded a few paces until she could hardly make out his face in the shadows. It would also keep Gideon from seeing the many emotions no doubt clouding her expression. "What does that mean?"

Gideon followed her as she continued to step back. His gray eyes were filled with the desperation and longing that had held her heart in a viselike grip all these months.

"I thought you dead, Gideon," she seethed. "I *convinced* myself that you must have perished, or else you'd be by my side. Surely, that was the only thing that could keep you from me." Her anguish seeped from her on a curt chuckle.

He shook his head, and his shoulders sagged. "I am not dead, nor would I choose to spend even a second away from you if I could have prevented it."

Gideon reached out to her as her back pressed into the wall behind her.

Music and the buzz of conversation floated from the ballroom on their other side.

Her mind was screaming just as loudly. Sybil shouldn't believe him. He was spinning a tale that would only serve to crush the small part of her that had survived his abandonment the year before. She could not risk allowing him close enough to hurt her again.

"I am not a dullard, my lord, nor am I a lady in need of a scoundrel," she hissed, ignoring his outstretched hand.

His intense stare pleaded with her to listen, to believe him. "It was never my intention to leave you,

Sybil. You must believe that."

"Then why did you?" It was the question she'd been burning to shout at him since she spied him in the ballroom; however, it came out as little more than a whisper. "Why did you abandon me?"

"I can do nothing now but offer my sincerest apologies."

"But no explanation?"

His hand fell to his side as his gaze moved from her face. "Perhaps one day. But for now, no, I have no explanation for my absence."

"Because, as you said, it wouldn't be *safe?*" He'd used the word a few moments before. Said he planned to return to her as soon as it was safe.

"I promise I will explain all as soon as everything is handled."

She scoffed. "Oh, my lord, I have witnessed firsthand how much you value your promises." Sybil crossed her arms, her fingers tightening on her upper arms to keep from reaching out to him. Even in her fury, she longed to touch him, to know he was real and unscathed. "Besides, I cannot guarantee I will be available to hear your explanation once the time presents itself."

Even as she uttered them, each word was like a knife to her stunted heart.

From the anguish clouding Gideon's stare, he was as deeply wounded by the words as she.

With a sigh, Gideon rubbed the back of his neck. "I have wronged you, Sybil. I know that. I will work every day to make amends, but you must understand, I had no choice but to depart London."

"And I cannot bring to mind a single reason that you could not have at least written me during all those—"

Gideon stepped closer, running his finger down her cheek to her neck as he leaned ever nearer. "You are, perhaps, more beautiful than that night outside my townhouse," he muttered, his gaze on her lips.

His warm breath caressed her skin, and she longed for his hands to do the same.

"Do not attempt to distract me, Gideon."

"My name has never sounded so sweet." His lips almost brushed hers with the final word, sending a strong shiver coursing through her. "May I kiss you, Sybil?"

"No," she murmured, but her denial was weak.

All he needed was to ask again, and she would agree, give him everything he longed for because she desired his kiss, as well.

But he didn't push her, only held his place, their lips so close his breath became hers.

She stared up into his face...a visage as familiar to Sybil as her own; yet his eyes were ringed with dark shadows, his face slimmer than before, and his cheeks hollowed. He'd lost a significant amount of weight since she'd last seen him. He did not just *appear* exhausted, he obviously was weary, as evidenced by the dip of his shoulders, his waxen complexion, and the grim set of his mouth. He was bone-tired—on the brink of collapsing. Not even newly tailored evening garb and a fresh razor could hide the fact that Gideon was drained.

"You haven't been sleeping well." She reached up and ran her fingertip along his face, his jaw tensing at her intimacy. "Are you in trouble, Gideon?"

She knew even without his answer that he was—in grave danger if his haunted look told her anything.

Over the last year, Sybil had endured near societal ruin. She'd been fodder for the gossips and all but crucified by Lady X's scandal sheet. However, Gideon's pleading stare told her that he'd been through much worse...yet, he returned to her.

The uptick of her heart spoke volumes.

Surely, Sybil could trust her heart, for if not, she had little hope she could survive should Gideon disappear again.

She loved him. And the soft pleading in his eyes said he felt the same about her.

Nothing had changed between them over the last year despite their hardship.

A door slammed, and Gideon stepped back, pivoting to face the sound, putting himself squarely in front of her. Peeking around him, Sybil spied a shadowy figure as it crossed the corridor and continued down the hall Gideon had traversed earlier.

"I should go." Even before the words had left her mouth, she was inching down the wall toward the door that would return her to the ballroom. "We cannot be seen here…together."

"May I call on you tomorrow?" He knew as well as she the power and destruction that could be caused if they were discovered alone in a dark corridor—the gossip sheets would not allow the indiscretion to go unnoted.

"You can do as you please, Gideon, but I must return to the festivities before anyone questions my absence." She stared up at him, her eyes begging him to make her stay; however, good sense won out for both of them. "Goodbye, Gideon."

"Goodbye, Sybil." He took her gloved hand and pressed his lips to it in farewell.

She pulled her hand from his hold, grabbed her skirts, and hurried toward the ballroom.

"Farewell, my love."

His words floated on the stale air, a crushing reminder of the last time Gideon had uttered that exact phrase. This time, she prayed it would not be so long until they met again.

CHAPTER 3

It is with the utmost curiosity that I must share with you all that was seen on the night of Lady Lichfield's birthday celebration. Namely, Lord Galway and Lady Sybil in an embrace most intimate and scandalous in the darkened halls of Lord Lichfield's townhouse. I must say that this sighting comes rather unexpectedly, as this author was preparing to announce the long-awaited betrothal of Lady Sybil to the Duke of Garwood. Is this pair—Galway and Lady Sybil—fated to be, or will the viscount disappear once more, as quickly as he returned?

~ LADY X, 25 March 1816

GIDEON GLANCED UP from the drying wax on the folded paper before him, long enough to nod at the servant standing at the edge of his desk, before turning his focus back to the note. Another moment, and the black wax with the Galway crest prominently displayed would be hardened and the missive ready for delivery. A large part of him was surprised that it had come to this, while a nagging thought remained that it was exactly as he deserved.

Holding the note out to the servant, Gideon instructed, "Deliver this to Oliver's Bookshoppe off Bond Street. Hand it directly to Mr. Oliver and no one else. Understood?"

His servant collected the note and tucked it into his jacket pocket. "Of course, my lord."

When the servant fled the room, closing the door soundlessly behind him, Gideon reclined in his seat, rubbing his face with both hands.

Two days.

Two bloody long days.

He'd promised to call on Sybil the day following Lady Lichfield's birthday celebration.

What Gideon hadn't counted on was Lord Lichfield, Sybil's brother, turning him away.

And now, he was forced to send a note by way of Sybil's favorite bookseller. Gideon wasn't even certain the man would remember what to do when the servant arrived at his shop.

Gideon had failed Sybil. Again. At least this time, it wasn't his fault, though that made it no less reprehensible. Perhaps he should have appeared on Lichfield's stoop and pounded on the door instead of sending word requesting an audience with the earl.

Scanning his desk, he grabbed Lady X's gossip sheet and skimmed down the page until he spotted the vile woman's latest on dit. Someone had indeed taken note of his and Sybil's meeting two nights prior, and they'd been kind enough to report it directly to London's most notorious scandalmonger. It wasn't the story on his and Sybil's intimate moments in the hall that angered him most, however, it was the fact that Lady X knew something Gideon didn't…something he never would have guessed.

Sybil was all but betrothed to another man.

A bloody duke, no less.

She hadn't breathed a word of it the other night. Not that he'd given her a chance to tell him. He read the name again, the Duke of Garwood. Gideon didn't know the lord, had never made his acquaintance and knew naught of him in general. Yet, he already disliked the man.

Perhaps he was unfairly judging the duke.

He certainly had superb taste in women if he'd set his sights on Lady Sybil.

He pushed to his feet, the chair beneath him groaning in protest as Gideon walked to the hearth and tossed the scandal sheet into the flames. Satisfaction filled him as he watched the words disappear as the paper burned, the edges curling in as the cream parchment turned black and then gray as it dissolved to ash. The words were not so easily forgotten, however, nor would the duke be banished just because Gideon threw the paper into the fire.

Everything had become clear once Gideon read the scandal sheet.

Lord Lichfield had no reason and, as a matter of fact, had a very *good* motive for turning Gideon away and denying him an audience. Sybil was all but betrothed to another. And Lichfield was likely quite pleased with his sister's ability to secure the notice of a duke as opposed to a mere viscount. Gideon had been foolish enough to think it had something to do with his disappearance before the contracts were signed for his and Sybil's betrothal.

Did Sybil love the duke?

If she did, Gideon would not stand in the way of what she wanted for her future or her happiness.

Yet, neither would he end his pursuit to gain back her affection so easily.

He'd slept in the hull of a pirated merchant vessel, eaten table scraps collected on the streets of Dover, and barely escaped before the hunters overtook him, Giles, and Charles in a tavern on the outskirts of Manchester. He had never been one to give up easily without a fight.

And Lady Sybil Anson was worth a thousand

battles.

She was the one thing that had kept him going all those months as they pushed from one place to the next. Outrunning the men who searched for them had been paramount, and he'd like to believe he did it to keep Charles safe, but the truth was, he kept going each day, knowing the time would come when he'd be able to return to London…and Sybil.

That day had come, but was he too late?

If their brief time together at the ball was any indication, he wasn't too late.

After he'd left the ball, he developed a plan. He would speak privately with Lichfield and tell him as much as he could without putting the earl in danger, and then he'd spend the rest of his life making amends for his disappearance.

Was it too much to hope that Lady X's latest gossip sheet would put an end to the Duke of Garwood's courtship?

Gideon hoped it would; however, he would only blame himself if it were at the expense of Sybil's reputation.

The shuffling of boots and the thump of a cane announced Charles' arrival long before he made it down the hall to Gideon's study with the help of a footman.

Turning from the fire, Gideon suppressed his own troubles as he called for his friend to enter.

"I hadn't knocked yet," Charles laughed as he walked across the threshold, assisted by only the cane. "How did you know it was I?"

In response, Gideon only lifted a single brow.

"Oh, this damned thing?" Charles lifted the cane and shook it. "If I weren't a burden before, this cane certainly makes my infirmity all the more obvious."

Gideon strode across the room and helped Charles to the large, overstuffed chair closest to the fire. If Gideon thought the last year was difficult, he could only imagine the horrors heaped upon his friend after being taken and forced into service nine years ago.

Gideon had given up one year of his life and returned whole. Charles, on the other hand, had forfeited nearly a decade and escaped, only to be crippled. Both in his mind and in his body.

"At least you no longer have to contend with the swell and dip of the ocean currents." Gideon sat in the chair beside his friend, savoring the comfort of having Charles back in his life. "I think, all things considered, you are luckier than most men."

Charles tossed his cane, and it skidded across the wooden floor until it hit the wall beside the hearth. "A damned inconvenience, I assure you. And a burden to you."

"That couldn't be further from the truth," Gideon said, staring into the flames. So many times, Gideon remembered that fateful night: two friends in London for the first time as men—drinking, carousing, and merriment. They'd been several ales in when the recruiter joined their conversation in the tavern. Gideon had known the area was unsafe, yet, he'd been convinced he was invincible in his youth. A turn about the docks had sounded like jolly fun. The man, a British naval recruiter, had tricked both Gideon and Charles that night. "You will remain here in London until I gain word from the Admiralty Court."

"And after that?" Charles asked, pinching the bridge of his nose. It had become a habit for the man, and he'd told Gideon it was the only thing that could stave off the headaches that assaulted him day and night.

Gideon clasped his hands in his lap. "You are free to remain with me in London, or retire to our childhood home in Northumberland." Neither of them would be traveling anywhere until Gideon had proof that no one searched for them. "Once I have word that there is no longer a bounty being offered for your return, it will be your choice what comes next."

Charles chuckled. "My choice? I'm the son of a steward—a commoner—with not a shilling to my name *and* a damaged leg. My choices are limited, to say the least."

"What is mine, is yours," Gideon retorted. "Everything. My homes, my coffers, even my stables."

"What happened wasn't your fault, Giddy," Charles said with a sigh. He leaned his head back against the chair and closed his eyes.

Gideon had always loathed the nickname his mother had bestowed on him during his infancy, and once he'd moved to London permanently, he'd thought the moniker forgotten. However, if it gave Charles some semblance of normalcy, then Gideon would gladly answer to *Giddy* for all his remaining days.

"We both know it was I who begged you to accompany me about town that night. And we also know that if I hadn't gone on and on about my status as a viscount's son, you would not have been targeted by the press gang because of your status as a steward's progeny." It was what he'd told himself all these years, and why Gideon had lost the need for boastful proclamation. His friend had been taken because the man at the docks discovered that Gideon was of noble birth, and therefore, out of reach. The British Navy needed sailors to fight in the colonies and against Napoleon, and they hadn't been against taking their own countrymen to fill the vacant ships. "It was because I dragged you to the tavern by the docks. Because I was an arrogant man in my youth. Because I drank too much and therefore couldn't fight off your captor."

Gideon paused, pushing from his chair and heading to the sideboard.

"It is not too early for a drink, is it?" Gideon didn't await Charles' answer but poured two tumblers of scotch. "Do not think I don't find the irony in this."

Handing the glass to his friend, Gideon lowered himself back into his chair. They both swirled the spirits in their tumblers, but neither drank.

"Irony in what?" Charles asked, sniffing the scotch.

"If it weren't for the scotch that night, you never would've been taken. Yet now, I drink to drown out the memories."

"If we hadn't been drunk, it is far more likely that they would have killed you, dumped your body in the port waters, and taken me anyway," Charles refuted. "They are a debauched lot without morals or manners to speak of. Many would slay their own mothers if their country asked it of them. They were simply doing their jobs."

"Doing their job?" Gideon scoffed. "They took you against your will. Your father was never the same after that. I think both our sires died of broken hearts—mine because my mother was gone, and yours because his only son disappeared."

"Again, not your fault." Charles downed his scotch in one long swallow.

It never ceased to amaze Gideon how compassionate and forgiving his friend was, especially following his years of forced servitude. He'd never blamed Gideon for his kidnapping. Truly, he didn't even cast a negative light on the men charged to impress men into service.

"Now, far more important than languishing on and on about my sad, pathetic future—" Charles held up his hand to stop Gideon. "Bad choice of words, my apologies. But that is not the point. What of the fair Lady Sybil?"

Gideon took a sip from his tumbler. The scotch burned as it traveled down his throat and warmed his uneasy stomach. "Her brother, Lord Lichfield, has forbidden me from calling on her."

"Forbidden you?" Charles chortled. "Impossible."

"Yet true, and within his rights as her guardian."

"And you are adhering to his edict?"

"Of course, not," Gideon said, holding out his

hand for Charles' glass. "Another?"

"Certainly. You drink to forget the past, while I imbibe to help clear my mind and bring into focus the future." Charles attempted to stand, but his leg was still too weak.

"No need to get up." Gideon moved to the sideboard and removed the stopper from the decanter of scotch. "I have sent a note to Lady Sybil. If it is her wish to never speak to me again, she will ignore it; however, if I arrive at the place I bid her to meet me, and she is there...I know not all hope is lost."

"If I were a betting man—which mayhap I am—I think she will be there."

Gideon turned from the sideboard and rested his hip against the table. "You have more faith than I, my friend."

"No, that is not it." Charles' expression turned severe, his mouth dipping into a frown, and his brow furrowing. "I listened to you speak of the woman for months. One cannot make up that sort of connection. She risked much to meet you the night you left London to find me. In my experience—"

"What experience have you?" Gideon asked, immediately regretting his words. "I mean to say..."

"Fear not. I am not offended." Charles sat forward, his intense stare holding Gideon's. "In my limited experience, it is not every lifetime a person comes to know someone as loyal, dedicated, and determined as you, Giddy. You searched for me long after I had stopped trying to free myself. If I am correct, you will not give up on your courtship of Lady Sybil any easier."

Gideon had not been completely forthcoming with Charles. Perhaps he didn't want to hear his friend's advice about the situation. Yet, the time had come to tell him the whole of it. "Lady Sybil is nearly betrothed to the Duke of Garwood. It might have naught to do with my determination, and all to do with where Lady Sybil's affection now lies."

"A healthy dose of competition?" Charles teased, taking the replenished tumbler from Gideon. "Come now, do you think this lord loves Sybil more than you do? Do you think he will be a better husband and father than you could be? Do you think he will provide the affection and stability you promised her?"

"I don't know the man from any other walking the streets of London," Gideon admitted.

"Let us take your heart out of the equation," Charles retorted, taking a sip of his scotch before continuing. "What does your gut tell you?"

His gut? Was it not only his heart that mattered in this type of decision?

"Rational thought, Giddy."

"I know I will cherish Lady Sybil all her days. I would dedicate my entire existence to her happiness, just as I promised before I left London. As far as Garwood goes, and his intentions, I cannot speak to that."

"Then I think it wise to speak of this with Lady Sybil when next you see her."

"I have never withheld anything from Sybil."

Charles raised one brow at Gideon's proclamation.

"Well, aside from my search for you."

"Perhaps she would have understood everything and not accepted Garwood's courtship had she known the whole story."

"I cannot tell her now," Gideon said with a firm shake of his head. "It would be too dangerous. If the bounty hunters find us and learn my identity before I receive word from the Admiralty Court, they could learn of my past connection to Sybil. They could hurt her to find us."

Charles lowered his gaze to his glass. "I think we evaded the hunters near the Scottish border nearly three months ago. I am not fearful that they will come here—to your home—and attempt to return me to the ship. Besides, the Villa de Constance and the Victoria have long set sail for parts unknown."

"Until I have the papers in my hands, officiated by my solicitor, I will not risk anything," Gideon bit out. "I will not put either you or Lady Sybil in jeopardy."

"Very well," Charles sighed. "But know this, once Lady Sybil and Garwood announce their betrothal, you will be gentleman enough to concede defeat. That much I know of you. You are an honorable man. If you love her, which I have no doubt you do, you must fight for her…and quickly."

Gideon had no need for Charles' warning. The precarious position he found himself in was at the forefront of his thoughts.

Both men fell into silence as their thoughts meandered and navigated their own musings—Charles' likely on his future, and Gideon's on a way to resolve his past.

CHAPTER 4

The end of the Season is upon us, my kind readers, and many debutantes have yet to secure so much as a second dance from a gentleman—much to the dismay of their marriage-minded mothers. One such lady we are all aware of is Lady Sybil. For the sister of an earl, she certainly has a way of frightening off eligible men. Lord Galway has not so much as shown his face in London in many, many months, and it is rumored that he took to the sea to be away from Lady Sybil.

~ LADY X, 9 August 1815

SYBIL PAUSED, TURNING her face toward the sun as it crested its noonday spot and started the fall toward the horizon. Her hands, though gloved, could still feel the smooth texture of the paper clenched tightly between her fingers in her cloak pocket. A note from Gideon delivered by Mr. Oliver. Smiling to herself, she nodded to a passing couple, adorned in their finest walking attire. The breeze was mild for spring in London, and the *beau monde* had escaped their stifling homes to bask under the warmth of the clear blue sky above. Women had set aside their needlepoint, and men of every status had forgone time secluded in their studies to promenade in London's fashionable Hyde Park.

On the surface, Sybil appeared like every other young woman enjoying her time outdoors with her parasol held high to keep the sun's rays from tinting her complexion. She began strolling once more, tilting her sunshade to block the light, and her maid fell into step a few paces behind her. She nodded to those she knew as they passed, either on foot, in open carriages, or on horseback. Keeping her steps unhurried, she moved down the walk until she reached the very end and pivoted to start back again.

Her maid leapt out of the way in response to Sybil's unexpected movement.

"My lady," Esther breathed, glancing past Sybil to their waiting carriage. "You have taken three turns. Is it not time we return home?"

"If your feet are sore, you may wait here." Normally, Sybil would not embark on any more walking than was socially called for during her early afternoon strolls. "I think I will have one more turn and then return home."

"I shall accompany you."

Sybil's hopes crashed at her maid's compliance. For the last hour, she'd attempted to tire her companion, but to no avail. The need to find other means of escaping her maid's watchful stare would be necessary. She'd brought a drawstring bag of tacks with her and was resigned to littering them on the ground if required; however, the thought of harming Esther just so she could slip away for a few moments seemed needless and cruel. It was not the girl's fault that she'd been asked to accompany Sybil on her walk. It had been Sybil's hope that Mallory, her sister-in-law, would come with her. The woman had a mind prone to distraction, and she'd likely not think much of anything if Sybil disappeared for a spell.

Sybil nodded to the girl and offered a small smile. "If you insist."

Bollocks.

Glancing up at the sun once more, Sybil noted that it was fast descending toward the tall buildings along the horizon. If she did not find a way to slip her maid's notice, she would be too late.

Once again, she passed the small trail that cut through a strand of overgrown bushes bordering the walking path. Consciously, she kept her eyes averted, not daring to glance down the almost hidden trail. It had been over a year since she had need to use it, following the path until the bushes receded and afforded a shielded spot if someone wished for a private moment in one of London's most visited parks. Obviously, it was only she and Gideon who knew of the secret spot as the bushes had grown nearly tall enough to block off the trail completely.

Sybil ran her gloved hand up and down her arm, her shoulders rounding slightly. Thankfully, she had no need to pretend more, producing goose pimples was beyond Sybil's abilities.

"Are you cold, my lady?" Esther asked, stepping to her side. "Perhaps we should return to the carriage before you fall ill."

Spotting a gathering of young debutantes not far ahead of her, their mothers gathered several paces away, Sybil waved to the group, slightly shocked that they, one after the other, waved back.

"Oh, what a pleasant surprise," Sybil cooed.

"You are acquainted with them, my lady?" Esther asked.

"Yes," Sybil lied. Lying was far preferable to physical harm, at least that was what Sybil chanted silently. "We met at Lord Gunther's musicale recital a few weeks ago. If you wouldn't mind, I wish to stroll with them while you return to the carriage to collect my wrap."

Esther glanced from Sybil's smiling face to the group of young women who'd returned to talking amongst themselves, Sybil forgotten. "Are you certain, Lady Sybil?"

The maid was rightfully justified in her concern.

"You'll only be a few moments," Sybil prodded.

She knew the instant the maid gave in—her shoulders hunched, and her frown disappeared. "I will find your wrap and hurry back."

"Very good," Sybil patted the maid's arm. "I shan't be far from this very spot."

She waved the maid off and turned to walk toward the women, but veered slightly after Esther was lost from sight. Certainly, she felt horrid about misleading the poor maid, but no injury would come to Sybil where she was headed; in fact, the area was safer than most places about London for the simple fact that only two people knew of its existence.

Sybil and Gideon.

They'd spent countless hours hidden from view as they spoke of their love, their future, and all they wanted from life.

It was only fitting that after breaking yet another promise to her, Gideon would request she meet him in their secret spot.

Glancing left and right, Sybil noted the young women had started off again, their backs to her. No one paid her any mind. She took a few steps back, making certain no one glanced in her direction as she made to adjust her glove before she ducked under the low-hanging branch and moved onto the narrow path.

A stick pulled at her skirts when she paused to close her parasol. Another branch protruded and nearly scraped her cheek. The ground was thick with fallen leaves and webs cascaded across the path, woven by spiders she'd rather not think about. Sybil barely stopped herself from rubbing the base of her neck as she felt something crawling across her skin.

Surely, she was imagining things. The topic of the human brain had been the focus of a scientific journal she'd found in her brother's study not long ago. The mind excelled at playing tricks on a person—made possible because who could know a person better than their own mind?

There was not a spider inching across her collarbone and slipping down the bodice of her gown.

Sybil pushed through the web blocking her path, a nearly invisible, dense strand of intricately woven webs, and hurried down the trail. She kept her parasol at the ready—just in case something larger than an eight-legged critter stepped in her way.

It only took a few moments—less than twenty paces—and she entered the small clearing, shielded by large bushes on all sides. The crunch of carriage wheels and light conversation floated on the spring breeze, but she could decipher none of the words. Just as if someone heard her speak, they would not be able to identify her voice or intuit what she said.

Anticipation coursed through her as she spun in every direction. The area was not large, there was no place to hide. Unmistakably, the small clearing was empty except for Sybil.

Pain gripped her chest at the same time sorrow shredded her insides.

She was too late.

The note had said noon. The midday hour had come and gone with Sybil attempting to outwit her trailing maid. She glanced up, but the shrubs stood so high they blocked the overhead sun. The time must be after one at least—an hour later than Gideon had bid her meet him.

Did he think she did not wish to speak with him after he failed to call on her the day after Mallory's birthday celebration? Certainly, Sybil had been angry and disappointed; however, that did not mean she would turn him down. There was still so much she didn't understand about the last year: why he'd left her, why he'd returned, where he'd been, and, most importantly, where did they go from here.

Had Gideon returned to renew their courtship, or only to give her a sense of closure?

She needed to know before her brother forced her to make a decision about the Duke of Garwood. He'd come to meet with Silas and had made it known that he was willing to wed Sybil and make her a duchess.

Willing to wed...yes, Silas had confirmed that was how the duke had phrased it.

As if she were a woman who needed others' pity.

As if she had no other recourse for her future.

He was *willing* to wed her.

The duke did not love her. There was no affection or even tender feelings between them. He would provide her with a home, an adequate allowance befitting a duchess, and in the future, a family. Any other debutante would have gladly accepted Garwood's offer of marriage.

But Sybil was not a debutante...and she'd known true love.

She'd tasted passion so strong her thighs quaked at the mere thought of it.

She'd had a desire sparked so hotly within her that the proposal of a loveless, passionless marriage of convenience held little appeal to her—less than little appeal. Absolutely, unequivocally *no* appeal.

She hadn't lied all those months ago. Even if Gideon were a blacksmith or a merchant's younger son, she would still love him. She would willingly give up the life she knew as the sister of an earl to be with him. The notion of raising a family in Cheapside or moving closer to the port area did not frighten Sybil because Gideon would be with her. He would protect her, care for her, and make certain they had everything they needed to survive.

That much she was certain of, if nothing else.

Yet, her faith in Gideon did not diminish her irritation.

Footfalls sounded on the path, leaves crunching under heavy boots as someone came toward her.

Had she been spotted ducking down the narrow trail? Was someone coming to see about her well-being?

The last thing Sybil needed, the very last thing her brother would endure, was another scandal.

It seemed her name—and that of her brothers— was forever linked to one scandalous escapade after another. Sybil had been mentioned so many times in Lady X's gossip column Silas had stopped berating her about it nearly three months prior. It might have had to do with his first mention in the sheet when he was turned away from Mr. Caruther's Shop due to Slade's mounting debts with the proprietor.

"Hello?" Sybil called down the shadowy path. If it came to it, she would claim she'd stumbled upon the trail unknowingly and taken it, becoming quickly lost. Then she would beg the intruder to show her the way back to the walking path. She'd bat her eyelashes and flash her most genuine smile if need be. "Hello. Please announce yourself."

When the footfalls continued without slowing, Sybil backed farther into the clearing. Not that it would save her if the person were bent on harm or scandal.

When Gideon stepped into view, she exhaled sharply.

Twice in as many days, she'd thought the worst of a situation, and both times, it had been Gideon who appeared. Peculiar that in both instances she'd been expecting him but feared it would be someone else entirely.

He took in her appearance from head to toe. "Were you expecting another?"

"Of course, not," she retorted. Her relief fled, and her ire returned. "It is only that I could not escape my maid for some time. I thought I was late, and you'd be gone already."

Gideon crossed the clearing, and Sybil waited for him to take her into his arms, pull her close, and gaze into her eyes. He'd done it so many times in the past that she could feel his strong arms around her. It had been a very long time since anyone held her—or made her feel loved and wanted. However, his hand did not reach to capture her. Instead, it tugged at her hair.

"Ouch!" Sybil batted his hand aside. "Whatever are you doing, my lord?"

When he raised his hand for her to see, he held a stick, complete with green leaves, between his fingers.

Sybil's face heated with embarrassment.

"You also have dirt on your cheek, and your skirt has a snag." A smug grin pulled at his lips, and he dropped the stick to the ground. "I suppose I should have surveyed the area before requesting that we meet here."

"Neither of us could have known," she said with a shrug. "Besides, a year does not seem enough time for such growth."

Sybil would not admit that the time he'd been gone felt closer to ten lifetimes to her.

"All the same, thank you for coming. I wasn't sure you'd get my note…or agree to meet." He stumbled over the words as his stare darted about the clearing. Gideon had never been an arrogant lord, yet neither had his confidence ever been lacking. This uncertain man before her was not the Lord Galway who'd left her all those months ago. He was different—unburdened but far from lordly.

How could a man raised in the upper crust of London society somehow lose his aristocratic air?

He was Gideon, the man she'd pledged to love until her dying breath, but at the same time, he wasn't.

"What happened, Gideon?" Sybil asked, her stomach twisted when his expression drew serious. Any hint of a smile was now gone.

"I requested an audience with your brother and attempted to call on you, but I was turned away," he admitted.

"Not now. I mean…what happened while you were gone?" Sybil watched him closely. If he wouldn't speak of it, at least she could gauge his emotional responses. "Was it another woman?"

She'd sworn never to verbalize her greatest fear, that Gideon had left for another woman. Briefly, there had been rumors that he'd cried off and fled London to be with another. Lady X's scandal sheets had blamed Sybil for his disappearance and called into question her standing as a lady of impeccable decorum and morals. It had nearly been enough to have Sybil requesting to journey back to Paris to live with her mother.

Gideon closed his eyes, turning sharply away from her. "Would it be easier to accept if it were?"

"Yes." *No.* If it were another woman who'd stolen him away, then it would only lead to Sybil doubting everything they'd ever shared—and the continued question of why he was back.

"I wish I could give you that answer, but…" His words trailed off.

It wasn't about another woman. He hadn't left her because someone else had captured his heart. There was a small measure of comfort in that, at least.

"Do you plan to leave again?"

"No, but not everything is within my control."

"What does that mean?" Sybil stamped her foot, and her knuckles turned white from her grip on the parasol. "I've grown tired of your riddles."

"I would offer you the world if I could. However, I do not seek to disappoint you again." Gideon pivoted and walked back toward the overgrown path. For a brief moment, Sybil feared he was leaving her again, that she'd spoken out of turn, and he was walking away. Turning back, he stalked through the grass carpeting the ground. "I can speak with Lichfield again. Request an audience and plead for forgiveness."

"I'm not certain that is wise, Gideon."

"Because of Garwood?"

Sybil shrank back at the name. Gideon knew of her courtship with the duke. She could see the hurt and betrayal in his stare.

"You were gone for over a year without a word," Sybil whispered. "There was gossip—"

"Yes, that I'd taken up as a pirate or made off to Gretna Green with another woman." He ran his fingers through his sandy brown hair, leaving it delightfully disheveled. "My favorite, I must say, was the report that I'd turned into nothing more than a common highwayman, terrorizing coaches from Dover all the way to Bath."

Sybil shook her head back and forth. "I never thought ill of you; however, I was also not certain you'd return. My brother, he—"

"Wants the best for you." Gideon halted before her, his eyes searching hers. "I have always wanted the best for you, as well. I thought it was I, but now...I cannot be so certain. Do you love Garwood?"

A bitter, stilted laugh bubbled up from deep inside her, filling the space around them with a crude sort of irritation. "How can you even ask that?"

"I must know, Sybil," he demanded, grasping the parasol from her hand a bit too forcefully and tossing it to the ground. "I needs must know where your heart lies. With me, or with this duke. I will not harbor any ill will toward either of you if you've found love in my absence, but I must know the truth."

Sybil wasn't prepared to speak on any matters of the heart, mainly because it was not only her thoughts that were confused and conflicted. Every inch of her knew she loved Gideon, yet why disclose it aloud if it led to further agony?

Guarded. That was how Garwood knew Sybil;

however, she hadn't always been that way.

Once, she'd loved openly and freely without fear.

It was not so anymore.

GIDEON STARED DOWN at Sybil. His Sybil. Kind, compassionate, with a hellion streak as long as the road to Edinburgh. His nights were filled with sweet dreams of her, held tightly in his arms. His days were unending hours of longing.

The long months without her had been torturous.

He'd never known her to do what was expected. And now was no different. He needed her to reassure him that things had not changed in his absence—that she loved him, and their affection for one another could flourish once more.

Sybil was not cursed with a tendency for hesitation.

It was what Gideon admired most about her. She knew what she wanted when he so often questioned his every decision.

"Sybil?" Gideon despised the begging note in his tone.

Leaving her as he had was wrong. He'd known it at the time; however, he'd thought the news was yet another wild goose chase, as all the ones before it had been. Two or three days away...that was how long he'd expected to be away from her. Enough time to journey to Dover, check on Giles' information, and return to London.

"The last year has been the hardest of my life," he confessed. More difficult than even those first few months after Charles was taken and Gideon had returned home to admit to both his father and Charles' sire what had taken place in London. Charles was gone—taken—and Gideon hadn't any idea where. "I truly long to tell you where I've been, what I was doing, and why I needed to stay away. However, I cannot speak of it yet. Just know that I thought of you...survived every moment away because I knew that one day I would come home to you."

Gideon ran his finger along her cheek, reveling in the feeling of her soft, warm skin against his.

For the briefest of moments, he thought himself too weak to keep his secrets from her. He could confess everything and know she would not breathe a word to anyone. Did they not hold many secrets between them?

Just as quickly, though, doubt set in. If he told her of his race across the country to rescue Charles, the many months spent moving from place to place as they eluded the hunters who trailed them, he would be putting her in danger. He and Charles had only retuned to London once they were confident they'd shaken the men following them; however, they couldn't hide forever. If the hunters learned of Gideon's identity, they would come to town and stop at nothing to take Charles back in order to collect their bounty—and his friend would be lost. Forever.

No, he couldn't speak a word of it to anyone until there was confirmation from the Admiralty Court. The paperwork that would ratify Charles' freedom from the press gangs. Making it so he'd never again need fear for his safety.

Until that day came, Gideon was sworn to secrecy.

"Gideon," she said, stepping back from his touch. "I must go. Esther will likely call for the watchman if I am away for another moment."

"Don't go. Please."

"I must." Sybil collected her parasol, brushing away the leaves that clung to the delicate lace fringe.

"Allow me to make amends, even if you do not seek to renew our courtship."

"I will speak with my brother," Sybil said. "He will see the error in turning you away from our home."

Why was Sybil willing to go to such lengths to mend the relationship between Gideon and her brother?

It was Gideon's place to rectify the situation, not hers. "That is too much."

"Do you love me, Gideon?" Her brow arched high as if she expected him to hesitate as she had.

"Of course," he confessed, throwing his arms wide. "I love you with everything I am."

She nodded, her decision made, though Gideon was uncertain what she'd silently debated.

"I will come to you after I speak with Silas."

"I will meet you—"

"No, I will come to your house."

"You cannot." Gideon vehemently shook his head. It was too risky for Sybil to be seen at his home— scandal notwithstanding. What if the impressment hunters had tracked Charles and Gideon to London? What if the Admiralty Court sided against Charles and came to collect Gideon as a treasonous man?

"Why ever not?" she demanded, her annoyance flaring once more.

Bloody hell but he'd missed her, far more than even he realized. She challenged him, pushed him to the limits of society's edicts, and had him questioning even his own decisions. How could he turn her away?

"Please, Sybil." Gideon closed his eyes to banish the images of Sybil arriving after nightfall on his stoop. She'd ask to enter, and he'd be helpless to refuse. "Things are not what they once were. We are no longer a courted pair. All of London is abuzz with news of your coming betrothal to another."

He couldn't bring himself to say the man's name aloud.

"It was not my decision to encourage Garwood's interest." Sybil pushed past Gideon toward the trail leading back to the walking path. "Nor will I entertain the courtship any further, my lord."

Without another word, Sybil started down the path, using her parasol as a walking stick as she jabbed the pointed tip into the ground, matching the stomp of her booted feet. Gideon might have been amused with her display of irritation, perhaps even called her back to make things right; however, it was not within his power to right anything.

He could not confess where he'd been all these months.

He could not tell her why she could not come to his home as she'd done so many times before.

He could do nothing but promise his love for her, and pray that one day, hopefully sooner rather than later, he would be free to explain everything.

The upward tilt of her chin as she marched out of view sent a shiver of unease coursing down Gideon's back. If there was one thing he'd learned about Lady Sybil Anson, it was that when she set her mind to something, her determination knew no bounds.

Gideon counted the long seconds until half an hour had passed since Sybil fled.

No matter what Sybil said, Gideon was aware that Lord Litchfield had an aversion to scandal, and if Gideon sought to court Sybil once more, it would serve him well to keep both his name and Sybil's above reproach.

Sybil had courted scandal more times than she'd had suitors.

But her ruination would not come by his hand.

CHAPTER 5

The lady loves a scandal. I assure you, my dearest readers, nothing can be closer to the truth about the Earl of Lichfield's sister. Many say it can only be attributed to her upbringing in France. After all, the French certainly have a way with theatrical wiles. Why ever would Lady Sybil put an end to the Duke of Garwood's courtship unless she had hopes of Lord Galway coming to heel?

~ LADY X, 30 March 1816

"YOU CANNOT DO this, Silas," Sybil shouted, the windowpanes rattling in their casing. "You are a brute, a scoundrel, a beetled-headed buffoon!"

"Sybil," Lady Lichfield hissed, setting her wine goblet on the table next to her. "That is not necessary."

Despite her sister-in-law's admonishment, Sybil kept her narrowed stare pinned on her eldest brother where he sat behind his desk, a fortunate place for him to rest else Sybil was likely to throw a punch at his perfectly sculpted jaw. The room spun around her, the warmth of the hearth heating her skin as the pungent aroma of cigars burned her nose.

Silas scrubbed at this face before lifting his stare to hers, his expression mirroring Sybil's narrowed glare. "You gave me no other option."

"France, truly?" Sybil demanded.

"We will be coming with you," Mallory insisted. "It will be a family adventure. My first trip to Paris. And I think Slade is amenable to the journey, as well."

"Only because his mounting gambling debts will see him in debtor's prison before the year is out." Sybil could not believe anything that had happened since she returned from Hyde Park. Determined to speak with Silas, she'd gone immediately to his study, only to have her path blocked by her sister-in-law. "Slade can do whatever he pleases, but when I desire something, I am reprimanded and sent away."

"You are not being sent away, Sybil." Mallory stood, moving toward her, but Sybil sidestepped the woman's touch. The last thing she needed was her sister-in-law getting one of her premonitions and sending Silas into a fit once more. "We will travel to Paris to visit your mother. Do you not miss her?"

"Missing my mother has nothing to do with this, and you both rightly know it." When Silas arched one brow high, Sybil knew she would let Silas win if she didn't get control of her anger. With a deep breath, Sybil calmed herself and started once more, "As I was saying, it is not my fault that Garwood has cried off. There was no official announcement, and the lord was a stuffy braggadocio anyways. He was more interested in hearing himself talk than listening to anything I had to say."

"Be that as it may, he has ended your courtship, but has agreed not to speak on the matter amongst society," Silas bit out, running his fingers through his onyx hair. "If we wish to say you decided to call off the coming betrothal, the duke is agreeable to that."

"Only because he would be labeled a scoundrel if the truth were known."

"You did not want to wed Garwood anyways," Silas refuted.

Sybil crossed her arms, tapping the toe of her boot on the carpeted floor. "That is neither here nor there."

"What is at the root?" Mallory offered.

"That I am the one being punished," Sybil sulked, unable to stop the whine in her tone. "I will be sent to France, and Garwood will be free to set his cap on another unsuspecting lady."

"Set his cap?" Silas asked. "You say that as if Garwood is a scoundrel, a rogue, and a dastardly lord."

Sybil lifted one shoulder. "As if I would know. He was in no way a master at conversation."

If her brother succeeded in dragging her to Paris, she'd never see Gideon again. She'd never determine where he'd gone or learn what had affected him so greatly that he returned a different man.

"What was my one rule during your debutante Season?" Silas pushed from his chair and walked purposely around his desk until he stood directly in front of Sybil. "What did I beg of you?"

"Not to create a scandal," Sybil muttered, averting her stare and tightening her arms across her chest.

"And what would you call this situation with Garwood?" he prodded.

"A fortunate turn of events," she whispered.

"Try again."

"An unfortunate turn of events?"

"Yes, very unfortunate, especially after that gossipmonger, Lady X, insinuated that you'd been seen—in *my* home—in an intimate embrace with Lord Galway." Silas's nostrils flared with each uttered word. "Can you imagine my surprise that just the other day, a courier arrived with a note from the absent viscount requesting an audience with me? With *me,* after he disappeared without a trace on the day we were to meet to sign the betrothal contracts."

Sybil wanted to correct her brother. Gideon had

disappeared the night *before* the contracts were to be signed; however, she knew it would be unwise to interrupt her brother at this juncture.

"Did you invite Lord Galway into my home without my knowledge or permission?" Silas queried.

"No." It was the truth. Sybil had been shocked to see that Gideon had returned to London.

"But you knew he had returned?"

"Of course, not," Sybil snapped, pivoting away from her brother's hard stare, fearful of what his next question might be. "I was utterly astounded to see him, but I will not say that it was an unwelcome surprise."

"We both know you loved Lord Galway very much…" Mallory allowed the words to trail off as if baiting Sybil into denying her true feelings for the viscount, or admitting that they'd changed in any way over the last year. "It is only that we never want you to be hurt again."

"You think Gideon has returned with the purpose of injuring me once more?" Sybil demanded.

"Heavens, no—" Mallory stepped to Silas's side and slipped her hand into his. "We do not think he ever meant to harm you—or your reputation. But his reappearance is suspect. Can you not agree?"

"I most certainly will not agree; however, I can confirm that if you make me leave London, it will be you—the pair of you—who is causing me pain. Not Galway or Garwood…you." Sybil started for the closed study door, determined to exit the room with her chin high. If she were to cry, it would be in the comforts of her private chambers, not before her brother. "I will bid you both good night."

"Sybil, wait," her brother called, the hard edge leaving his voice.

"Dear brother, I can assure you that the only thing we will never learn is why Gideon fled London because you turned him away when he requested an audience," Sybil hissed, refusing to turn back to face Silas. She would have liked to see his expression when he discovered that she knew of his refusal to meet with Gideon; however, she knew tears were not far away. Allowing Silas to witness how gravely she was affected by Gideon's return would be unwise.

"What am I to do with you, Sybil?" Silas sighed in defeat. "What will you have me do to fix this muddled mess we find ourselves in?"

"Have a bit of faith in Gideon, even if you cannot trust in me."

"Sybil, your brother loves you dearly," Mallory countered.

"Not enough to allow me to experience an ounce of the happiness he has found," Sybil said, fighting to keep her voice from cracking. "Good night."

She raced from the room, slamming the door in her wake. She'd been a fool to think that Silas was capable of allowing her the freedom to choose her own path in life. He'd found love in a most unexpected way with Mallory—along the shores of Bocka Morrow in Cornwall during the Christmastide Season, no less. They'd had nearly five years with one another, experiencing all that marriage offered a wedded couple…while Sybil remained alone. Why could her brother not see that she had also found love in a most unexpected way?

The implications and repercussions of Silas's decision to remove Sybil from London would have dire consequences for them both. She was not fighting to be allowed to see the latest onstage play at Covent Gardens. This was not an inconsequential squabble over an increase in her allowance. It would be difficult, likely impossible, for anyone on the outside to see the difference. She'd done just as she had when she was younger—she'd screamed, she'd belittled, and she'd argued until she was in tears.

Stumbling down the corridor, Sybil entered the servant's stairwell and climbed to the second floor where the family rooms were located.

The hall was deserted with only two sconces to light her way.

She passed Silas and Mallory's chamber and halted before Slade's door. No light shone from beneath. Her brother—Silas's twin—could not be more different than his identical counterpart. Where Silas was rigid and demanding, Slade was uninhibited and insouciant. Silas adhered strictly to societal norms, while Slade flouted convention.

If she had to place herself in the mix of her family, she would fall as a cross between her two brothers. She was loyal and independent, much like Silas. Though she did not always think that conforming to society's rules over her own desires was a wise thing.

Sybil knocked on Slade's door, but her brother did not answer. He was likely not in residence, choosing to spend his time about town, doing as men were allowed: whatever suited them.

Perhaps Sybil should do the same.

Slade had amassed a sizeable gaming debt in the last few years; however, Silas did nothing more than scold him, and he never failed to settle the debts when they were called in.

Could Silas's threat of returning her to France be nothing more than that—a simple edict he had no plans to follow through with?

Either way, Sybil was free of Garwood and their attachment.

Even though Silas was not agreeable to discussing a renewed courtship between her and Gideon, Sybil had no qualms.

When her brother had spoken of removing her from England and dragging her across the channel to France, the only thing she'd thought about was Gideon. Her heart still belonged to him, no matter how much she tried to convince herself otherwise.

Even if Silas would not hear Gideon out, Sybil

could, and then she'd attempt to change Silas's mind. Her brother had to see reason.

With one final glance at Slade's door, Sybil turned and continued on to her room. If Silas were unwavering in his course to ruin her future, and Slade wasn't home to assist her, she needed to find her own way to secure the outcome she desired.

The night was still early, only two hours after nightfall. Gideon had bid her not to go to him, but if her brother was serious about her departing London, then she needed to speak with Gideon.

Where he'd disappeared to last year didn't matter.

What he continued to hide from her, while irritating, did not change the way she felt about him.

Together, they could work through everything that stood in their path, Silas included.

Gideon loved her, he'd told her as much in the park. Yet, she hadn't been able to tell him in return. She'd been confused and hesitant, but their impeding separation made everything clear.

Sybil desired Gideon in every sense of the word— his heart, his body, and his forever.

She loved him, and she'd be damned if she would allow anything to stand in the way of what she wanted.

Scandal be damned.

Gideon Lyndon, Viscount Galway, belonged to Sybil, and no one, not the London gossips or her brother, would tell her differently. Even Gideon himself was in the wrong, thinking he could keep her from going to him.

Slipping into her room, Sybil hurried to the dressing closet to make certain she was alone—which, indeed, she was. Her maid had already turned down her bed and disappeared for the night. Had the entire staff gotten word of the duke crying off?

That was likely the second-best thing to happen to her that day, number one being Gideon sending word to meet him at Hyde Park, at their secret spot known only to them. As if nothing had changed, the months melted away, and she'd rushed to meet him, not knowing what to expect. Instead of declaring his love once more, he could have broken off their association, pushed her to wed Garwood, and said his final goodbye.

Her anger and irritation—the months of unending gossip at her expense—did not hold her any longer.

Sybil loved Gideon, and she'd been a fool not to tell him—letting him believe his feelings weren't reciprocated.

Without a moment's hesitation, she gathered her cloak, muff, and wool scarf, and retraced her steps back to the servant's stairwell, pausing briefly at Slade's door. Still, no light shone from below, so she exited the townhouse through the kitchen and slipped into the dark alley beyond.

CHAPTER 6

London is quiet with so many seeking their country homes for the Christmastide and New Year's holidays; however, this author witnessed quite a display of family quarrels—in the middle of Bond Street, no less. The Earl of Lichfield, with his wife and Lady Sybil in tow, was turned away from Mr. Caruthers's Shop due to an unpaid bill by none other than Mr. Sladeton Anson, the earl's twin brother. I do not think this will bode well for finding Lady Sybil a suitable husband…yet, much will be forgiven and forgotten by the time Parliament resumes in the new year.

~ LADY X, 22 December 1815

THE SUDDEN HEAVY pounding that echoed throughout Gideon's townhouse brought a sudden panic to Charles' stare as both men set down their utensils and gazed at one another silently across their plates. Despite the roaring fire in the hearth, stoked at least twice an hour, Charles wore a heavy blanket around his shoulders to ward off the chill that his friend said clung to his bones far more adamantly than a mutton chop.

Gideon had only briefly experienced the frigid night air when he was made to sleep outdoors during the time he and Giles searched the docks for the ship that kept Charles captive. His friend spoke of weeks and months at sea, sleeping on the open deck when the roiling of the ocean permitted, and how the frothy salt water had seeped through even the heaviest of garments.

The fires in every hearth would remain burning hot every day for the rest of eternity if it brought even an ounce of comfort to Charles.

The knocking receded, and Pires, the Galway butler, shuffled by the dining hall toward the foyer.

Apprehension marred every line on Charles' once boyish face.

"I have given my servant specific instructions that no one is to pass my threshold without my explicit permission," Gideon said, nodding at their meal. "I am not expecting anyone. Therefore, we shall finish our repast undisturbed."

The tension did not leave Charles, but he followed Gideon's lead and took hold of his knife once more. He cut a piece of duck into minuscule portions before bringing a bite to his mouth.

Gideon had taken great pride in watching Charles gain weight and strength as each day passed. His skin no longer had the yellow hue of sickness, nor did his fingers shake when he brought his glass to his lips. Yet, still, the haunted stare remained. Gideon wondered if it would ever disappear completely, even when official word came from the Admiralty Courts declaring Charles a free man.

"What if they send orders demanding my return to the *Caledonia*. Or, worse yet, send the pressmen?" Charles' head hung as he made a show of staring at his plate, his knife moving a roasted turnip from one side to the other. "I shouldn't have accepted your offer of lodging. I have put your entire household in danger."

Gideon's chest tightened with fear, though he refused to let Charles notice his trepidation. "It is highly unlikely that a man in your condition"—Gideon gestured toward his injured leg nestled under the table—"would be found useful on a warship."

"There are many tasks aboard a ship that one does not need the use of his legs to successfully accomplish." Charles had spoken of this exact subject several times when Gideon had hired a physician to examine his friend and submit a written report to be included with his paperwork sent to the Admiralty Courts. As well as when Gideon had several pairs of trousers commissioned at his tailor's, and even that very morning when Gideon had bid Charles accompany him to Hyde Park. "They may not demand my return to a ship, but they could turn me over to the courts for judgment."

Gideon had long since run out of encouraging words to ease Charles' fears. "We can only wait until word arrives with regards to your fate."

While Charles had little confidence in the outcome of his friend's request to the courts, Gideon was positive that Charles would be released from his impressment duties. If Charles' injuries were not persuasion enough, Gideon was prepared to offer a large sum to make certain Charles' bounty was paid.

Gideon would buy his friend's freedom a thousand times over if that was what it took.

Being of noble birth, Gideon had never known the fear of being pressed into service to the crown. Neither of them could have imagined the consequences of their blithe night of drinking by the docks. To think that they could awaken and have their lives be utterly unrecognizable hadn't crossed either of their minds. Gideon because his station in society placed him above such things. And Charles because he'd trusted Gideon.

A faith that had been obviously misplaced.

However, Gideon would not fail Charles again.

"My lord," Pires cleared his throat at the door. "A

missive arrived for you."

Gideon waved the servant closer and snatched the letter from his hand, immediately noticing the distinctive seal of the courts. Maritime tradition boasted the silver oars as the symbol of their authority.

The audible gasp from across the table said that Charles had seen it, too.

"I hadn't expected a response so quickly," Charles said.

Gideon met Charles' gaze. "I didn't either. My solicitor, who has an old friend in the courts, said it could take up to a year to hear anything on the matter."

An entire year during which time Gideon had been prepared to keep Charles hidden and safe.

A year before he could speak on the matter to Sybil, and that was if he could remain in her good graces for that extended period of time.

"Are you going to open it?" Charles rearranged the blanket covering his legs, attempting to hide his nervousness regarding what the letter held.

Gideon extended his arm, holding the letter out for Charles to take. "I think you should do the honors."

"It is addressed to Viscount Galway, not me," he said with a firm shake of his head.

They both stared at the letter, Charles not making any move to take it, and Gideon wondering if he dared to open it. They'd waited less than two weeks after his solicitor delivered Gideon's request. Did the court's rapid response signify that they were in agreement with the laws governing the Navy's ability to impress men into service with no notice?

The practice was barbaric—and archaic.

There were men of every station about England who longed for a commission into the crown's Navy; yet during the wars, his country had continued with the practice of forcing unwilling countrymen to serve.

"My lord, my apologies for interrupting your meal once more, but we seem to have a situation in the front drive that needs your attention," Pires said with a curt bow before hurrying back to the foyer.

Gideon's first thought was that the courts had sent men to collect Charles and remove him back to the port immediately.

"I will come with you." Charles laid his napkin on the table beside his half-empty plate, and a footman stepped forward to assist him in standing. "My cane, if you please, Jackson."

"You should wait here." Gideon knew his request would be met with defiance.

Charles was resolute in his decisions, much like a certain dark-haired, wild-spirited woman Gideon was acquainted with.

"If they are here to collect me, I will go willingly." Charles held his chin high as he collected his cane and started for the door. "I will not cause you any more grief."

The only person responsible for Gideon's surmounting grief—with accompanying guilt—was Gideon himself. It had been his fault that Charles was taken, and now, Gideon had once again not done everything in his power to protect his friend.

"They will not take you," Gideon bit out through clenched teeth, taking hold of Charles' arm as they walked side by side toward the foyer. "That much I can promise you."

"We may not have a choice."

There were always options, of that Gideon was certain.

"—you will allow me entrance."

Gideon's steps faltered as the familiar voice floated down the long hall.

"Lord Galway is expecting me," Lady Sybil said, her voice rising an octave.

"My lady, I can assure you, the viscount is not—"

"If you would announce my presence, I can *assure you* Gideon will welcome my arrival."

"Who is that?" Charles asked, hurrying his steps while Gideon dug in his heels. "It cannot be…"

Gideon released Charles' arm, and his friend shuffled ever closer to the foyer, his injured leg dragging slightly in his haste to find out what all the commotion was about.

It was on the tip of Gideon's tongue to call to Charles, warn him that the woman might be a distraction, a ploy to get Charles out into the open so he could be apprehended.

"Giddy, is that who I think it is?" Charles hissed in his direction. The words echoed in the foyer, bouncing off the vaulted ceiling. "Lady Sybil Anson?"

He saw enough to notice that Sybil had stopped tussling with the footman who attempted to keep her out of the townhouse.

"Step aside, my man, step aside," Charles' voice boomed across the foyer. "Allow the woman in. Have you completely forgotten your manners?"

The elder of the pair, Gideon had forgotten Charles' assertive nature from their boyhood days. His commanding voice and sturdy presence dominated every village gathering at Gideon's country estate. As they aged, Gideon had no doubt that the young women of the village would just as likely find delight if asked to dance with Charles as they did with Gideon.

The footman stepped aside, and Sybil huffed as she pushed the hood of her cloak back and began unbuttoning the long row of brass buttons holding the overgarment closed to keep the chilly night air at bay.

"Very kind of you, sir," Sybil said, turning her most innocent smile on Charles.

Gideon watched the man practically melt into his boots.

"As I was attempting to tell Lord Galway's butler…"—she paused, glancing about the foyer—"wait, speaking of Gideon, where is he? And who are you?"

He could fairly visualize Sybil's confused expression—the way a single cocoa brow would raise, her lips would press into a frown, and she'd stumbled over her words. None of this would take away from her exquisite beauty. It would only serve to lull Charles into a false sense of chivalry. He would want to help her, assist her in any way possible, just to dispel her unease.

"I am Mr. Charles Smythe." With amused chagrin, Gideon watched Charles bow grandly as if Sybil were the queen. "Lord Galway and I grew up together. My father worked as the Galway steward for several decades."

"It is a pleasure to make your acquaintance, Mr. Smythe."

"Do call me Charles."

If anyone in Gideon's household thought it peculiar that Lady Sybil had arrived at Gideon's door—obviously unchaperoned and long past the socially acceptable calling hour—they did not breathe a word of it.

At that moment, Sybil glanced over Charles' shoulder, spotting Gideon lurking down the hall, her eyes narrowed on him.

"We were enjoying our evening repast," Charles said, nodding back down the hall. "Would you care to join us?"

"I...well...I came to speak with..." Sybil stumbled over her words as she glanced between Gideon and Charles. "I suppose I should join you, or I fear your food will grow cold."

Gideon had remained hidden long enough. Stepping into the foyer, he greeted her. "Good evening, Lady Sybil. I was not expecting you. In fact, I believe I specifically said not to—"

"Heavens," Charles snapped as he held out his arm for Sybil. She glanced at it for only a second before determining the man posed no danger and set her fingers at his elbow. "It appears everyone in this household has abandoned their manners. Luckily, I am here, the perfect gentleman."

Sybil giggled. Actually giggled.

In the last few minutes, Charles had gone from utter terror at what the letter held to charming London gentleman.

It was obvious his friend had missed his calling. Sybil's radiant smile as she stared up at Charles sent a jolt of pure jealousy through Gideon. Odd how the appearance of a beautiful woman had them both forgetting the letter from the courts.

Gideon slipped the missive into his shirt pocket and followed the pair as they walked by him toward the dining hall.

"Jackson," Gideon called to the lingering footman. "Please, have a place setting added for Lady Sybil. She will be joining us for the remainder of our meal."

CHAPTER 7

Another woman? Tell me, kind readers, that this author is mistaken. It is rumored that Lord Galway did not leave to pursue his interest in pirating, nor did the intrigue—and coin—of a life as a highwayman steal him from our great town. No...another woman? I shan't believe it until I see it with my own eyes.

~ LADY X, 3 January 1816

SYBIL DID HER utmost to remain tranquil and composed at Gideon's dining table as the man to her left, Mr. Charles Smythe, regaled her with tales from the viscount's childhood by the Scottish border. Inside, she was reeling from the fact that Gideon had such a close confidante and friend he'd never spoken of to her.

Smiling and nodding, as any enthralled woman would do while listening with rapture to the men jesting back and forth, Sybil could not help casting furtive glances in Gideon's direction.

It was with great abandon that she'd told Gideon everything about her past—before he learned of her less than stellar upbringing in France in the gossips—yet, he'd kept so much of who he was and where he came from to himself.

"...and so, Giddy and I—"

"Giddy?" Sybil asked, raising a brow at Gideon. "I must say, I have never heard anyone call Lord Galway *Giddy*."

To his credit, Gideon's cheeks flamed, and he made at least an attempt to look sheepish. "Yes, it was what my mother called me when I was very young. A play on Gideon, obviously, but also because I was fond of horses."

"And he'd neigh before he spoke," Charles laughed. "He not only had a fondness for horses, but he actually thought himself one until he was what..." He paused and looked at Gideon for input, but the viscount remained silent. "Age fifteen?"

"Come now, Charles," Gideon boomed. "It was closer to five."

"All right, all right...I find myself exaggerating the details for the amusement of our guest." Charles laid his napkin next to his untouched plate. "I find I am helpless to do anything but make certain Lady Sybil is having a marvelous time after her less than hospitable welcome."

"I assure you, Charles, my arrival was a shock to everyone, including Lord Galway." Sybil saw Gideon cast his friend a veiled glance as she tried to make excuses for him. "Besides, my mere presence here is highly scandalous, do you not agree?"

Sybil took a sip from her wine goblet to keep from glancing in Gideon's direction. She knew bloody well he was angry with her. He'd specifically instructed her not to call on him, but what other choice did she have? Gideon was keeping things from her, and she doubted Charles' presence at his townhouse was even the half of it.

"I can only speak to what I see, my lady." Charles gestured to the pair as he spoke. "I see a dour, slightly distracted lord, having a pleasant meal with a beautiful, articulate woman while chaperoned by a dashing young man of little consequence. Though I've been away for some years, I do think this meal will hold up to even the highest scrutiny."

"No one shall know about this meal." Gideon pushed back his chair, a footman jumping in to assist him as Charles followed suit. "Lady Sybil, will you be so kind as to join me in the study for a private conversation?"

Charles tsked. "That, I'm afraid, will not hold up to any—"

"Charles." The warning in Gideon's voice halted his friend. "Lady Sybil?"

A footman pulled her chair back, and she smiled at both men. "Of course, my lord."

Could it be that she was enjoying this? Gideon was rather irked, and Charles was doing his utmost to prod him.

Sybil was familiar with the many sides of Gideon: reserved and pensive, light and jesting, confident and chivalrous.

But this demanding, domineering, stalwart man before her was different.

"If I have angered you, Gideon, I am sor—"

"My study, Sybil. Now." He didn't wait for her, but pivoted and stalked from the room.

When she turned to Charles with a weak smile, he only shrugged, but his following wink settled a bit of her unease at Gideon's turn in demeanor.

"It has been a pleasure meeting you…far overdue, if you do not mind my bluntness," he said with a stiff bow.

She didn't mind his candor at all. "May I offer a bit of frankness?"

"Certainly."

"Why have we never met?" Her tentative question brought a shadow to the man's face. "What I mean to say is, Gideon and I have known one another for quite some time, and he has never so much as mentioned your existence."

Sybil expected hurt or at least confusion to cloud Charles' face; however, his expression turned dark, and he pivoted to the footman for his cane, not looking back at her when next he spoke. "I think that is something you must speak with Gideon about. I bid you good evening, Lady Sybil."

He hobbled from the room, his cane hitting the polished floor the only sound as she was left in his wake.

Bloody hell. She didn't know where Gideon's study was located.

As if sensing her flustered temperament, the butler stepped into the room. "My lord is awaiting you. This way, please."

When he gestured for her to follow, Sybil moved around the table, quickening her pace to keep up with the servant.

Sybil was uncertain why she was annoyed. A private moment with Gideon was the reason she'd flouted convention and dared come to his townhouse.

Perhaps it was that her arrival had only added more questions to the surmounting concern surrounding Gideon's return, not even to touch on his disappearance. If she were to convince her brother that dragging her back to France and away from the man she loved was a bad idea, Sybil needed answers, not more questions.

The door to the study stood open, and Sybil spied Gideon pacing before the hearth, his strides long and heavy on the carpeted floor. There were not many occasions when she had the opportunity to gaze upon him unnoticed. His sun-kissed light locks hung over his collar in a very pleasing manner. How had she not noted that his hair had lightened significantly over the last year, as if he'd spent months in the sun? His cream-colored skin was several shades darker, making it contrast considerably with his hair. His skin tone did nothing to hide the dark circles under his eyes, however. Had he not slept recently? He'd appeared unburdened when she spotted him at the ball several nights past, but a weight had obviously settled upon him since she first laid eyes on him again.

She was desperate to know what troubled him, and how she could help.

But he'd need to open up to her first, trust her with whatever he kept secret, and have faith that she would do her best to assist him.

His shoulders tensed, and he halted, staring into the open flames. It tore her heart from her chest to see his frame snag as he exhaled.

"I told you not to come here." His tone held little conviction. "It is dangerous."

"Mr. Smythe does not seem at all perilous," she whispered as she stepped into the room. She paused for only a moment before turning to close the door behind her. "And we both know what I think of society and its need for scandalous on dits."

Gideon turned to face her as the latch clicked into place.

They were utterly alone, and the way his gaze traveled the length of her before settling on her lips told Sybil he was all too aware of it, as well.

For once, Sybil did not have the urge to run into his arms, to press her body against his, to have his lips warmly caressing hers. To completely lose all of herself in him; his smell, his hold…his heart.

"Damn it, Sybil." The palm of his hand landed on the stone edge of the hearth, and he turned to face her, his eyes alight with something akin to chaos. "How am I to protect you when you embrace peril at every turn?"

Disarray. Turmoil. Utter pandemonium.

Gideon's narrowed glare held it all.

"I have survived nearly twenty-three summers without you sheltering me; in fact, I lived nearly an entire year thinking you were dead, gone, never to be seen again. Why did you not protect me from that?"

"I left you a note."

"Excuse my lack of decorum, but a bloody note scribbled upon crumpled paper, closed with a lopsided seal...it did nothing to assure me that you'd return."

"I could not tell you where I was going and had no idea how long I'd be gone."

"Just as you still cannot trust me enough to share where you were all those months." Sybil said the last word as her breath ran out. She drew in air deeply, ready to launch into yet another volley of questions and concerns, but she got no further than, "I cried myself to sleep for months, Gideon."

"Hurting you is something I will apologize for endlessly; however, I can make no amends for leaving that night." He ran his fingers through his hair, his long locks hanging askew from the action and matching his wild-eyed stare. "I had no other choice."

"If you have returned, why am I still in danger? Who poses a risk to my safety?" she begged. "I am no one of import."

"You are of *great* import to me!"

The words should have filled her with a sense of security, to know that she meant something more to him than the last year had shown. Instead, the volatile lilt to his tone had her flinching away.

"I love you, Sybil, and there are people...if they knew how much I cared for you...they would seek to harm you if only to get something from me."

"Does this have to do with Charles?"

"Yes," he said with a sigh, slumping into one of the two chairs facing the fire. Sybil moved into the room and sat on the other seat, her stare mirroring his as they both watched the flames licking at the logs. "He was taken...years ago. It was my fault."

Taken? "Do you mean kidnapped?"

"Kidnapped, impressed, tied, bound and gagged." His lips pressed into a frown. "Call it what you want, but he was taken when I should have protected him, watched over him, and made sure he returned home safely."

"Where did they take him?" Sybil wasn't sure she wanted to hear any more, but she suspected this was the heart of Gideon's secret…and she would know it.

"To sea." Gideon's head hung as if the entirety of the blame was his to shoulder. "We were in London, directly after I finished University, and I convinced Charles to spend an evening out and about London, doing as boys who think they are men do—drinking and carrying on."

He fell silent, but Sybil didn't prod him for more. He would speak when he was ready.

Finally, he pushed to his feet and strode to the sideboard.

"Pardon my horrendous manners," he called over his shoulder as he took the stopper from a decanter and poured a drink. "I have spoken of this to no one in many years."

"I will have one, too," she said.

His back straightened, but he removed a second tumbler and poured her a small portion of scotch before returning to his seat.

"We were both so deep in our cups that we stumbled to yet another tavern, this one far too close to the docks, and a man bought us another round of drinks." He took a sip from his glass, his eyes staring unseeingly into the hearth as he re-lived the moment. "We were young with no funds to our names other than what our fathers gave us, and we'd spent that far earlier in the night. So, we accepted the drinks without question. The next thing I knew, I was waking up in a rubbish heap with the sound of the lapping waves on the dock pillars causing my head to swirl and my stomach to churn."

"What of Charles?" she asked in a breathless whisper.

"Gone." Gideon leaned forward, setting his empty glass on the table between their seats. "Taken without a trace. It took me a fortnight to learn what had happened to him and where he was likely headed."

All manner of notions collided in her head: taken by the magistrate, imprisoned at Newgate, banished to the colonies for some sordid crime.

"He was snatched up by a press gang and forced into service on the Centurion for our Royal Navy. From there, he was traded from ship to ship, whenever the need for sailors shifted when the entire British forces were sent to handle Napoleon and his troops."

"You could not have known…"

"Do you want to know why they didn't take me, as well?" Rage seethed with each word. When Sybil could only nod, he continued, "My dress was that of nobility, while Charles wore the simple garb of a commoner. I was spared because of my father's wealth, while Charles was imprisoned on ship after ship, forced to sleep in the elements, eat stale, moldy food, and contend with cruel abuse because his trousers were not snug enough to give the impression of station."

"But he has been rescued," she ventured. "He is home…and free."

"That is the thing, he is not free." Gideon glanced at her hands, still holding the scotch he'd given her. "He is still in danger, as am I for forcibly removing him from a Navy vessel in Dover. We are hunted men, and if we are found before the Admiralty Courts have had time to decide on the matter, he will be returned to the ship, and I could be punished."

Sybil indignation flared. "But I would not allow that to happen. My brother would champion your cause. We would fight until you both were freed."

Gideon snorted. "Lord Lichfield will not so much as entertain an audience with me. What leads you to believe he would put his own reputation on the line to save me?"

"Because he is a good man, an honorable one, a lord who prides himself on his loyalty."

"He owes me no loyalty, Sybil," Gideon sighed. "I made a promise to you, and to your family, and I abandoned that promise."

"With good reason," she retorted.

"But Silas doesn't know that."

"For the sole reason that you haven't explained it to him." Sybil took a small sip from the tumbler clutched between her bone-white knuckles, thankful for the burning respite as it made its way down her throat to her stomach. "And, he may owe you no amount of loyalty; however, as I said, Silas is an honorable and good man, and he has been known to dote on his sister. If I asked it of him, he would go to the ends of the Earth to see me happy, especially if it meant saving the man I love."

His inquisitive gaze captured hers across the space that separated them.

Her words shocked her as much as they did Gideon.

Embarrassment flamed, and her face heated. "It was not my intent to speak out of turn, Gideon. I know now is not the time, but—"

"I love you, too, Sybil," he said, his stare never wavering. "That is the one thing that has never changed, even with all the secrets I had to keep from you, and the time away with no explanation. I hoped every day you'd forgive me...and love me still."

"While losing you hurt me, it did not stop my heart from longing for you."

"As I have pined for you." Gideon stood, pacing before the hearth. "I dreamt of you every night, Sybil. I told myself that if you ever forgave me, I would never cause you another day of grief. Yet, here we are."

He said everything Sybil had longed to hear him say: that he'd missed her, he'd thought of her, and he loved her.

A heavy, persistent knock thundered through the townhouse, so close, Sybil thought it was someone at the study door. The thump rattled the windowpanes at the same time the tall clock began to chime the top of the hour. Her hand shook where it clutched her tumbler, sending the liquid over the rim and onto her gloved hand, marring the delicate satin.

"Bloody damnation!" Gideon hissed. "This night has had no end of visitors. Not that I was unhappy to see you, Sybil."

"I did not take offense." Sybil cleared her throat and set the glass aside before standing. "I suppose it is time I return home before it is noticed that I am gone."

Gideon pinched the bridge of his nose as the hammering on the door continued. "I will have my carriage readied. If you'll wait here, I will take care of it and see why no one has answered the damned door."

As he left the room, a dark cloud descended around him, and tension tightened his shoulders, evident even through his evening jacket. A large part of her wanted to follow him, to ease whatever caused him worry; however, he'd bid her to remain, and for once, she was resigned to listen.

Was it that she didn't want to leave? They'd only just begun discussing the many things that had kept them apart, caused them both immeasurable pain, and found common ground—the one thing that kept them together.

Love.

Gideon left the study door wide open after departing, his footsteps muffled by the incessant knocking at the front door as it drifted and echoed into the room Sybil waited in. Who could it be at this time of night?

Finally, the butler must have opened the door because the knocking suddenly stopped and the halls of Gideon's townhouse returned to their quiet ways.

"Where in the *hell* is my sister, you chutless, fobbin

codpiece?" Silas's enraged voice boomed through the house, causing tendrils of dread to course down her back.

Her body shook with fright. Never in all her years had she witnessed Silas in such an angry state. She'd gone against her brother's precise wishes by going to Gideon when he'd forbidden it.

"Let us step outside and speak like gentlemen," Gideon retorted in a much calmer tone; however, she knew Gideon's patience would only last so long, especially if her brother continued on with his name-calling. "I am certain we can rectify whatever slight you think I've committed."

Sybil moved to the doorway and peered down the hall toward the foyer. She couldn't see her brother's face and only had a clear view of Gideon's back, his shoulders stiff and his chin raised.

"You've single-handedly ruined my sister," Silas continued. "We should meet outside; however, dawn is a preferable time…and Regent Park an adequate location."

Was Silas challenging Gideon to a duel?

Sybil couldn't wait around to find out. She needed to stop the two men she loved from harming one another with anything deadlier than their words.

Rushing from the study, her half boots made no sound as she ran toward the foyer.

CHAPTER 8

A stalwart magistrate, an incessant earl, a not-so-innocent maiden, an unsavory Jack Tar, and an indignant—yet furious—viscount…tell me, kind readers, what these five have in common. There is no rhyme or reason to any of it. However, that was the scene, which took place outside Lord Galway's London townhouse. This author wonders if the next we hear of it will be at dawn—with pistols!

~ LADY X, 3 April 1816

"LET US TAKE matters outside," Gideon said once more, his voice boomed as if thunder had erupted in his home. However, it brought Lord Lichfield and the man who'd accompanied him to a standstill. He wasn't certain that moving their confrontation outside was any better, but at least it would not be handled in the presence of the fairer sex. "I am certain we can discuss this matter without being driven to violence."

Lord Lichfield scoffed. "I should have pursued you all those months ago when you disappeared, leaving my family to shoulder the burden of scandal."

Sybil's brother pivoted and walked out the door, then, the other man following closely on his heels. Could Gideon get away with slamming the door shut, throwing the latch, and sneaking Sybil out the back door to the stables, returning her home safely while her brother waited outside Gideon's townhouse?

That thought was dashed when Sybil appeared at his elbow, slipping her hand into his as she started for the door. Gideon was helpless to do anything but follow her lead.

"You should wait inside." Gideon drew to a halt and turned to face her. "Allow your brother and me to speak privately. I may be able to change his mind about us."

He looked down into Sybil's brown eyes, like melted chocolate as the candles from above danced over her face. "Can we not attempt to change his mind together?"

Perhaps with Sybil present, her brother would be less prone to violence and more likely to remain calm and listen. However, glancing out the door, Gideon saw that Lord Lichfield hadn't made it but a few steps and now faced him and Sybil, his hands on his hips and his boots shoulder-width apart. If his stance weren't evidence enough of his fury, then the tightness in his jaw and his noisy, labored breathing was sufficient to give Gideon pause.

"Brother," Sybil said, donning her most innocent smile as if they were welcoming Lord Lichfield for morning tea. "However did you find me?"

"It wasn't difficult," Silas snorted. "I know damned well when I forbid you to do something, it is exactly what you will do."

"Forbade me to see Gideon? Oh, you did far more than that when you threatened to send me back to France." The pair glared at one another, and Gideon was hesitant to interrupt. Their expressions said a war of words and wit was eminent; however, their tone remained cordial. "Whoever"—Sybil paused, her stare going to the man at her brother's side—"is your friend?"

The man, dressed much like many solicitors and businessmen Gideon had encountered, blinked several times before speaking, "I am the Honorable Mr. Augustus St. Paulson. Magistrate for the Westminster borough."

"A magistrate?" Sybil pulled Gideon ever closer until he felt the length of her pressed to his side. "But we haven't done anything wrong. Have we?"

"He is only here to make certain you are returned to your family without controversy."

"Returned...you say that as if I have been taken," Sybil countered.

"Well, how were Slade or I to know you *hadn't* been taken against your will?" Lord Lichfield asked.

"I can assure you, she was not."

All heads turned toward the door where Charles stepped outside, his cane firmly in hand.

"Who are you?" Lichfield demanded.

"Mr. Charles Smythe—no fancy title or court appointment." He strode forward to join the group, taking up a place to the right of Sybil as he addressed the magistrate. "May I give my accounting of this evening's events? I am certain you will see that there was nothing untoward or criminal about Lady Sybil Anson visiting Lord Galway."

"I suppose that is the way of things." Mr. St. Paulson pulled a small notebook and pencil nub from his jacket pocket and nodded to Charles. "I am ready."

Charles cleared his throat, adjusted his neckcloth, and tapped his cane tip against the cobbled driveway. If they'd been anywhere else, if the matter at hand weren't so grave, and if Gideon hadn't been staring straight into Lord Lichfield's enraged eyes, he might have chuckled at his friend's display.

"Now, Lord Lichfield—henceforth known as the

aggrieved party—has no legal standing as Lord Galway—now known as the...well, for lack of a better term since my mind is failing me, the *comforted* party— did not allow the fair Lady Sybil Anson into his home, I did. When she appeared on his stoop, he did as any gentleman would: he welcomed her into his home after I allowed her entrance. He even provided her with a meal, until, you, Lord Lichfield arrived to collect her. Should he have sent her into the cold, dark, dangerous night?" Sybil chortled, but Charles' serious stare had her quieting. "I dare say, it is Lord Lichfield who has been negligent when it comes to the welfare and well-being of his sister by allowing her, unchaperoned and unprotected, to gallivant about London—"

Lichfield's nostrils flared with indignation. "I will have you know—"

"Enough," Gideon called, slashing his hand through the air. "I have heard quite enough, Charles, but thank you. And magistrate, Lord Lichfield could no more have kept Lady Sybil in the safety of her home as I could have discouraged her from coming to my townhouse. She is a woman with her own mind, and she does not take kindly to anyone, especially me or the earl, commanding her about." He paused to take in Lichfield's reaction. While he looked a bit less enraged, his shoulders were still tense, and his fingers balled into tight fists. "However, it is that mind that has stolen my heart completely. I was helpless to turn her away when she appeared earlier, though I knew I should have loaded her into my coach and delivered her home immediately."

"It is what any gentleman worth his salt as such would have done," Lichfield seethed. "And now, my sister is ruined. Her reputation is in shambles, and there is no one to blame but you, Lord Galway."

Gideon's chest seized at the earl's harsh tone. He'd wronged and failed so many people in his short life— Charles had been taken, the elder Symthe had died before Gideon brought his son home, Sybil had been mocked and scandalized by his disappearance, and now, he was ruining her all over again.

He owed everyone present an apology; most of all, Sybil, for hers was truly the only opinion that mattered to Gideon.

Without a second thought, Gideon turned toward her, taking both of her hands in his as the cool night breeze ruffled her cloak hem and played with her long, brown tresses. "Lady Sybil"—Gideon held her gaze, fearful to look away—"I intended to arrive at your family home as planned to sign the contracts that would bind us as surely as a wedding ceremony. However, things beyond my control—beyond *anyone's* control—took me away from London for over a year. I failed you, and I failed your family, but I saved my dear friend."

Charles clapped Gideon on the shoulder, but still, he would not take his stare from Sybil's. He needed her to know and understand—even if her family was unwilling to listen—that he realized he'd disappointed her but was determined to make amends.

"I promise you, Sybil, that I will do all in my power, from this day forward, to prove to you how sorry I am that I failed you. To show you each and every day that my love for you is true and never waning."

Tears glistened in Sybil's eyes, and Gideon feared for a brief moment that he'd upset her again, caused her some unintended hurt or anguish.

His heartbeat sped up until he felt the rush through his entire body. "While I owe your family much for protecting you when I could not—especially from the London gossip my disappearance caused—it is now I who should care for you." Gideon squeezed Sybil's fingers before bringing her gloved hand to his lips. "Lady Sybil Anson, I have loved you since the day we met. I loved you when miles and circumstances kept us apart. I will love you more and more each day until my last dying breath steals me from this Earth. Will you do me the extreme honor of becoming my wife? My viscountess?"

Gideon sucked in a deep breath and waited, the moments ticking by as they held one another's gaze. It was no longer Gideon who held her stare, but Sybil making it impossible for him to look away. Without her, he would surely crumble. If she rebuffed his offer, Gideon would not likely survive it. He would be broken, ravished, and unable to go on.

"Well, it appears Lord Galway has satisfied his obligation to correct his slights against this woman's honor in the eyes of the law," the magistrate murmured.

Lichfield stomped his foot, taking a step closer to his sister. "Like bloody hell—"

"Yes, Gideon," Sybil sighed. "I will wed you. For my love never diminished either, not even in your absence."

Gideon gave a hoot of joy and swept Sybil into his arms—Lord Lichfield be damned—and swung her around. He hadn't been sure she'd agree to wed him again, especially after everything he put her through.

"I do believe a kiss is proper…to *seal the deal* as one is wont to say," Charles called with a laugh. "Come now, Lichfield, you should be happy. Now, you only have that blackguard, Sladeton, to see married. Your responsibility is half completed."

Gideon chuckled as he halted, Sybil settling before him as she reached up on tiptoes to place her lips against his.

She pulled back quickly, her cheeks flaming at the intimacy displayed before so many. "Gideon, I never doubted this day would come."

"The moment we would be standing in my drive in the middle of the night with your brother spitting mad, Charles prodding on his anger, and a magistrate present?" Her eyes twinkled as she nodded, her mouth pulling into a wide smile. "Well, I can assure you I never imagined a day such as this."

The thunder of hooves stampeded down the road beyond, the beasts turning into Gideon's driveway as the riders pulled to a halt and leapt from their mounts.

"Bloody hell!" Lichfield shouted as he stepped before his sister.

Gideon did the same, pushing Sybil behind him as the pair of newly arrived men sauntered forward.

"What is the meaning of this?" Gideon called.

"We be here on official-like business for Mr. Charles Smythe and Viscount Galway." The men moved close enough to Gideon for him to take in their attire: threadbare, short trousers, and coats that had seen many days at sea. The salty smell of the open water emanated from the pair as their beady, narrowed eyes trained on him.

"What is your business with them?" Charles asked. "Not that we know where they are, mind you."

"Mr. Charles Smythe be a deserter—a treacherous crime ta be certain," one of the men offered as he ran his hand through his oily hair. "Viscount Galway is ta face charges of aid'n 'im. Both be deemed capital crimes."

"Capital crimes?" Sybil pushed from behind Gideon and marched forward until she stood nose-to-nose with the man who'd spoken. "Surely, this is a jest."

The color had drained completely from Charles' face, and his hand trembled where he held his cane. They'd both known capture was possible, and understood that the punishment would be severe if they were found, but they'd come so far, even spotting a bright light of hope in their futures.

Sybil had agreed to marry him.

But before anything could be done, he was to be ripped away…again…with little chance of returning to her.

"I am Charles Symthe," his friend stepped forward. "I will go with you willingly."

"What is going on?" Lichfield demanded. "No one

is going anywhere. Not until I find out what this is about."

The earl looked between Gideon, Sybil, and Charles, waiting for someone to speak.

"Lord Galway disappeared last year because of me," Charles offered. "I was taken and impressed into service during the war. My ship ported in England, and when Gideon got word, he came for me. If anyone is to blame, it is I, Lord Lichfield, not Gideon."

"I not be care'n who's ta blame." The sailor glanced at his mate and nodded toward Charles. "We'll take 'im and come back for the other. Cap'n will be happy nuff with that."

"You cannot take him." Sybil lifted her chin as if daring the men to go against her wishes. "I will not allow it."

"Move out o' the way, ye Friday-faced light skirt," the sailor spit out. "We haven't the time for ye meddle'n."

Gideon had known Sybil to be headstrong, but her bravery bordered on insanity. The men before her were hardened sailors, likely killers where the need arose. Yet, she did not back down when the oily-haired seaman took a menacing step toward her.

Gideon's heart froze in his chest as if a sudden ice storm assaulted his entire body, keeping him from moving even the barest of inches. Only feet separated him from Sybil, but it might as well have been the English Chanel.

The sailors both angled their bodies toward Sybil, their narrowed stares enough to bring most grown men to their knees in fear, except Sybil made no move to back down. There was no chance Gideon could reach her before one of the men made to strike her.

CHAPTER 9

All's well that ends well...as the saying goes. I have it on good authority that London will shortly see another wedding shrouded in scandal and mystery with no small amount of intrigue! This author would swoon, but my latest headpiece would not survive the fall, I assure you. I reported over a year ago that the fair Lady Sybil Anson was to wed Lord Galway and, dear readers, I am never wrong.

~ LADY X, 10 April 1816

SYBIL IGNORED THE shiver of apprehension that coursed through her as one of the men attempted to grab her arm with his filthy, calloused, ungloved hands. Deftly, she sidestepped the sailor but did not allow them a clear path to Charles.

In an instant, Gideon was by her side, prepared to protect both Sybil and his friend.

How had she ever thought Gideon a scoundrel? He would gladly sacrifice himself for his friend, and Sybil knew that if she were to fall into evil hands, he'd be there to rescue her, too.

"Do not lay a hand on the lady," Gideon thundered.

"Step aside. We be collect'n what we came for."

"You will not be leaving here with anyone." It was Silas's deep, stern voice that voiced the words, his tone brooking no argument. He'd stepped forward to stand on the other side of Sybil, making it three people the sailors would need break through in order to get to Charles. "I require your papers, gentlemen."

The pair glanced at one another when Silas held out his hand and waited, wiggling his fingers to emphasize his demand.

"We not be need'n ta prove anythin' ta the likes o' ye." The sailor stood his ground, folding his arms across his chest and spitting at Silas's feet. "This be a court matter."

All eyes moved to the spittle that clung to the toe of her brother's polished Hessian.

"Gentlemen—and I use that term rather loosely…" Silas smiled. It was the same grin Sybil was known to have when she was up to something. "Allow me to introduce the Honorable Mr. Augustus St. Paulson. He is a magistrate in good standing with the courts of England."

"This be maritime law, ye bloody nob." Both sailors chuckled, thinking they'd outwitted Silas, but Sybil suspected differently. Her brother rarely embarked on a task unless he was certain he held the upper hand. "Now, move aside already before we be put'n a fist ta ye chin."

"Without any paperwork on the matter, you are trespassing on my property," Gideon replied, sending a conspiratorial glance in Silas's direction.

At some point, things had altered between her brother and Gideon. They'd gone from foes to allies in the blink of an eye. They now had a common objective.

Justice, fairness, loyalty.

Honor.

"Mr. St. Paulson, what say you?" Gideon nodded at the magistrate.

The tall, lanky man swallowed, adjusted his cravat, and cleared his throat—an obviously redundant gesture that filled Sybil with no assurance that the man was up to the task of his position as magistrate.

"We not be care'n what this jackanape be think'n, do we, Donovan?" the man who'd attempted to grab Sybil asked his partner, his lips pulling wide in a grin that showed his rotting teeth. "Been chase'n this swab all 'cross the country, we have."

"While I am well versed in the law of the land, I find my jurisdiction to impose rules does not extend to maritime law and that of the British Navy. However, if you have not brought with you any written notice to apprehend and return Mr. Charles Smythe, gentlemen, then I cannot, in good faith of the law of this great land, allow you to leave with him in tow." The words left St. Paulson on a long exhale, and the man's shoulders caved in after he'd stated his piece.

Sybil couldn't help but wonder what the magistrate would do if his words were challenged.

"As we said, we ain't got no paperwork," the sailor, Donovan, argued.

"We couldn't read it even if'n we did," his conspirator muttered.

"Then it appears you have no standing here." Silas clapped his hands, signaling the end of it all. "Gentlemen, it is time you depart."

The sailors glared at Silas and Gideon, but never did their eyes meet Sybil's. They knew they had no recourse to collect Charles, though they were having a difficult time accepting the fact.

On each side of her, Sybil felt the coiled strength of her brother and Gideon—the man she loved—ready to do battle if it came to that.

"Gentlemen, let us retire inside," Sybil called to the

party at large, lifting her chin a notch. "These fellows are leaving, and I will not have this day marred by bloodshed. It is not every day a woman accepts the marriage proposal of the man she loves with all her heart."

Gideon and Silas held their ground until the seamen mounted their horses and fled the drive, while Sybil led Charles and Mr. St. Paulson inside. She didn't pause until they'd entered the study she and Gideon had been in earlier. A servant must have tended to the fire while they were outside, and a refreshment cart with cakes and steaming tea had been rolled close to the sideboard.

She couldn't help but smile as she offered both men drinks and food while they waited for Silas and Gideon to join them. She hoped that their alliance had been solidified in an unbreakable manner. Sybil had no intention of departing England or turning away Gideon's offer of marriage.

In fact, Sybil was past the age of needing her brother's approval to wed, and with the magistrate present, the matter could be handled with a swift edict from a court official. It had been Silas who'd brought the man when the entire situation should have been handled privately amongst their families.

Her stomach twisted at the mere thought of needing to go to such great lengths to prove to her family that Gideon was the man she chose to spend the rest of her life with.

She handed both men cups and small plates filled with delicate pastries and sandwiches and they settled, the magistrate taking a straight-backed chair away from the fire while Charles sank to the lounge, propping his cane against the wall. Helping herself to a plate, she lowered to sit beside Charles as he stared silently into his cup.

"Charles?" she asked. "Is there something else I

can get for you?"

His eyes lifted to meet hers, devoid of the good spirits he'd shown at their meal, and Sybil couldn't help but feel a measure of sorrow for him. Imagining the horrors and pain he'd suffered during his forced years at sea was something Sybil simply wasn't prepared for. That did not mean she could not offer him comfort and a kind ear if needed, however.

"Lady Sybil, you—as well as Lord Lichfield—have been gracious enough this night." Charles shook his head, the action sending several droplets of tea over the rim of the cup and onto his bare hands. However, he did not seem to notice the hot liquid as he next spoke. "I had no intention of bringing any danger to you, my lady, and I pray that you and your family can forgive me."

It startled Sybil to realize the depth of Charles' guilt. "No harm came to me, and even if it had, I would still have been there to stand up for you."

"Gideon and I waited many months to return to London"—Charles paused, grinning over at Sybil—"and my dear friend droned on and on about you every day. I nearly fled in the middle of the night to be away from his tales of love, and the fables of your beauty."

Sybil laughed along with Charles, content to know that, once again, Gideon had been nothing but truthful with her.

"However, your beauty and steadfast, loyal nature are far beyond anything he shared." Charles brought his cup to his lips and took a long, slow sip, his eyes drifting closed as he drank. "I am so happy that my dearest friend has found you. He deserves to be loved and cared for, especially after so many years carrying the burden of my abduction on his shoulders."

"He never spoke of you to me before today. Not even the day he fled London," Sybil confessed. It was her turn to look away, not having the strength to meet Charles' stare. "Why do you think that is?"

She needed to know—did Gideon not trust her?

When Charles sighed, Sybil feared the worst. Gideon may love her, but he might never share with her his deepest moments, thoughts, and concerns.

"Over the years, Gideon scoured both England and Scotland in search of me. He had men stationed at every port, watching and waiting for any sighting of me. He'd had so many false reports over the years…so many times he'd hurry to Dover or up toward Edinburgh only to have his hopes dashed." With his free hand, Charles rubbed at his leg, likely to soothe the chronic pain from his injury. "Disappointment, guilt, and shame are powerful, all-consuming emotions. To be honest, I don't think Gideon ever thought to see me again. Not truly. Why would he mention his greatest failure—his words, not mine—to the woman he adores?"

"If a person loves another, they do not cast blame so out of hand."

Charles chuckled, a bitter, heavy sound that attracted the notice of the magistrate where he sat on the opposite side of the room. "The blame had already been cast, so in a way, he was keeping from you anything that could tarnish your love for him."

Sybil lowered her voice to a whisper. "Do you blame him for your capture?"

"Heavens no, my lady." Charles set his cup on the table beside the lounge and stared into the crackling hearth. "Even the day after I was taken, when I awoke at sea with England long out of sight, I did not lay the burden on Gideon. We were men, young as we were at the time, and the gang could've taken either of us or both of us. I was the unlucky one; yet, I was the mere son of a commoner with no future except what Gideon's father had promised me. Gideon and his family could afford to lose me, but Gideon…Gideon was, *is* destined for greater things."

"Because he is titled?" Sybil squeaked, the

implication angering her. To think that one man's life was any more important than another's solely because of their status at birth...it was inconceivable. Yet, it was everything England was built upon.

"Partly." Charles' candid confession brought a new anguish to her. "However, that is not the only reason. Gideon is a good, honorable, kind, and compassionate man. He will take his place among the men shaping this country for generations to come. He will *do* good, far more than a man such as I could ever hope to achieve."

"I cannot believe that, Mr. Smythe," Sybil refuted.

"That Gideon is honorable and kind?"

"No, that your life is less meaningful than Gideon's." Why did saying the words cause her heart to hammer in her chest? Could it be because she'd been raised to believe that the life of a nobleman was worth more than that of a commoner?

"I am not saying that either," Charles said, patting her hand.

Two sets of footfalls sounded in the hall.

"Please, Lady Sybil, do not punish Gideon for keeping my existence from you." Charles pushed to his feet and collected his cane. "He never meant to hurt you. I will bid you good night. I believe the matter to be discussed is a family issue."

"You are Gideon's family," Sybil said with a shrug. "I maintain that you have as much right to be here as I...and I can state, with certainty, that Gideon and I will be lucky to have you in our corner."

Both Gideon and Silas strolled into the room. Gideon's eyes surveyed the space until they landed on her, and he visibly sighed with relief. Her brother went directly to the magistrate.

"Mr. St. Paulson," Silas called, waving the man from his seat. "What is Mr. Smythe's recourse at this juncture if the men return?"

Gideon reached into his jacket pocket. He retrieved a sealed note and held it out for Silas and the magistrate to see. "This will resolve all the confusion."

"The letter from the Admiralty Courts." Charles shuffled over, taking the missive from Gideon and turning it over in his hands as his forgotten cane fell to the floor.

"You had this all along?" The magistrate's brow rose high in question. "Why did you not speak of it sooner?"

"We haven't opened it yet," Charles confessed.

"It arrived only moments before Lady Sybil. If we had opened it before the men, and the courts demanded Charles be returned to his ship, they would have taken him straight away, and any hope of petitioning the courts in appeal would have been difficult." Gideon nodded to the missive. "Open it, Charles."

"I think it best that I depart. As a member of the courts, I will be honor-bound to adhere to the Admiralty's directives." Mr. St. Paulson gave a curt bow to Sybil and nodded to the occupants at large before hurrying from the room as if the fires of Hell were chasing him.

Gideon and Charles remained focused on the official seal of the maritime courts.

"Open it," Sybil prodded. "Even if the news is disparaging, there is still time to appeal the decision."

Gideon stepped to Sybil's side and placed his hand on her waist, waiting for his friend to break the seal and read the notice. Even Silas waited in silence, a nervous air about him, though the outcome did not affect him as it did the others.

Charles slipped his finger under the flap, and the wax seal cracked, pieces falling to the floor at his feet. Unfolding the paper, he scanned it, his expression in no way betraying what news the letter held.

Finally, he held the paper out to Gideon, his hand shaking slightly.

Sybil held her breath as she read the words that

drifted across the page with perfect penmanship.

Tears clouded her vision, and it was difficult to make out the words, but a few phrases became seared into her mind, *relieved of duty* and *free from impressment*. Sybil's thoughts swirled as she tried to make sense of everything.

"I'm not to be returned," Charles announced, whether for Silas's benefit or Sybil's, she was uncertain. "I am officially free and need not fear anything further."

Gideon embraced his friend, each clapping the other's back before stepping apart once more. The relief was written clearly across Gideon's face when he returned to her side, pulling her close.

"Lord Lichfield." Gideon turned to address her brother. "Charles' freedom means mine, as well. I can pledge that nothing will come before Sybil. My time and focus will no longer be torn between the two people who mean the most to me. My love for Sybil has been in the forefront since the day we met; however, that did not stop my other responsibilities from taking me away from her and London."

Sybil silently pled with Silas to hear Gideon out—his intentions, his commitment, and his heart.

"Silas, I love him," Sybil said on a cry.

Her brother scrutinized Gideon from head to toe before returning his gaze to her. "Love—his or yours—is not what is in dispute here."

"Then, what?" Sybil's heart splintered at the thought of being separated from Gideon once more.

"It was I who had to comfort you when Lord Galway cried off and disappeared—"

"He did not cry off," Charles scoffed.

Silas turned his narrowed stare to Charles, his severe look quieting the man. "It was Mallory, my wife, who stood outside Sybil's door every night and listened to her cry herself to sleep." He turned to Sybil. "As your brother, your protector, I never want another to harm you. I will not stand silently aside again and allow any man—or woman—to speak ill of you, to fail you, to...*abandon* you!

"I am your brother, damn it. It is my duty to protect you from injury."

Sybil's hopes crashed as Gideon stepped from her side. Was he accepting defeat? Was he resigned to allow Silas to dictate their future? No matter how misguided his intentions were...

"Silas, please..."

"Let him speak," Gideon whispered close to her ear.

Gideon hadn't abandoned her, only moved to stand behind her as his hands now rested on her shoulders.

She didn't want to listen to Silas list all the reasons Sybil shouldn't love and wed Gideon. Her brother's reasoning mattered not a whit to Sybil. She knew her heart. She had witnessed Gideon's pure love.

And that was enough for her.

"Before tonight, I was against you wedding Lord Galway. Not because I feared the sincerity of his love, but because I could not trust him to be there when you needed him most," Silas sighed. "I will not always be close at hand to make certain you are well, that your children are cared for by a loving father. And that, rightfully, concerned me. As your brother and guardian, it is my responsibility to make certain you are wedded to a fine man, an honorable male, someone who will put you first forevermore."

"I am past the age of needing—"

Silas held up his hand to halt her words. "Until this night, only a short time ago, I truly believed that man was not Lord Galway; however, after witnessing the lengths the viscount was willing to go to in order to protect a friend, I believe he would do the same for you—perhaps better than I."

Sybil's shoulders trembled, her hands rising to rest

on Gideon's at her shoulders. "Are you saying…?"

"He has agreed to our marriage, Sybil," Gideon murmured in her ear.

She turned to face Gideon, her hands landing on her hips as she stared up at him. "How long have you known?"

"We discussed it outside as we made certain the men departed." Gideon smiled, and her irritation fled as warmth filled her. "The contracts will be drawn up in the morning, and we are to sign them by midday."

Sybil could barely believe what she was hearing. She and Gideon were to wed—with her brother's blessing.

"Good thing you've seen reason, Lichfield," Charles grumbled. "If I know anything about Gideon, it is that he will go to the ends of the Earth for those he loves."

"And I do love you, Sybil." Gideon's stare held hers, and he leaned down, placing a chaste kiss to her lips. "I am, here and now, making it my life's mission to prove to you, each and every day, that I love you."

"I never doubted your love," she confessed.

Sybil could not look away from Gideon. Every secret, every concern, every doubt had been exposed. There was nothing and no one who could stand in the way of their happiness.

"I think it best we depart," Charles' voice sank through Sybil's supremely happy musings.

"Not quite yet," Silas answered. "Galway, I trust I can expect you to arrive at the appointed time tomorrow?"

"Nothing will keep me from finishing what I started," Gideon said, his stare never leaving hers. "Above my honor and my duty, it is my heart that is forever pledged to you, Lady Sybil."

"I love you, Gideon."

Sybil vaguely heard a door closing behind them as her brother and Charles left; however, when Gideon's lips pressed to hers once more, she was helpless to think of anything but the man she loved.

Sybil could admit that she loved a scandal, and no scandal would capture society's attention more than the betrothal of Lady Sybil Anson to Viscount Galway.

EPILOGUE

It was a romantic, magical, and dreamlike soiree. All that was missing was cherubs or, mayhap, winged fairy creatures. I am certain even I would have fallen in love with the gallant Lord Galway had I seen him dressed in his wedding finery before his heart was given to Lady Sybil—now, Viscountess Galway. I can confirm that the only scandalous occurrence was Mr. Sladeton Anson leaping from the second-story window in nothing but his undone trousers. But that, my kind readers, is a story for another day...

~ LADY X, 28 October 1816

SYBIL TOOK A deep breath and smoothed her hands down the front of her freshly pressed white muslin nightshift as she stared at the closed bedchamber door.

Her new bedchamber door.

The room she and Gideon would share as a newly wedded couple.

In this space, adorned in deep, midnight blues and soft, creamy whites, they would make love for the first time. They would laugh with unfettered abandon, and discuss current events from politics to fashion and war. They would argue over topics as mundane as what to eat for their evening meal and debate important subjects such as what they would name their future children. Rupert, Melvin, and Gertrude were not names she was willing to entertain for their forthcoming offspring, no matter that they were established names in the Galway viscountcy.

All of those matters dealing with her new marital status were things that Sybil looked forward to experiencing—with Gideon by her side.

There was no doubt in her mind that, if they remained steadfast in their love and stayed committed to one another, they would see each other through both the good times and the bad.

And, at that precise moment, Sybil was preparing for one such good time.

She and Gideon had been wed that morning, followed by a feast with a surplus of food and drink, and a ball held in their honor. There was dancing, more refreshments, merriment, and good cheer all around.

A shiver coursed through her when footfalls sounded in the hall outside her—*their*—bedchamber door.

Gideon had arrived.

Her husband was directly outside the room.

Sybil smiled, pushing the last remnants of apprehension away as the latch sprang and the door slowly opened without a sound.

"Viscountess Galway." His voice was a heady whisper that sent tendrils of need coiling in her stomach. He was still outfitted in his wedding day finery, complete with polished boots and precisely combed hair. His gray eyes sparkled in the dim lighting from the dozen candles positioned about the room. "I have waited long to address you as such."

"Viscountess Galway." Sybil allowed her formal

title to roll off her tongue and hang in the air separating them. "And you, Gideon, are my husband."

Their eyes clashed from across the mere feet separating them.

It no longer felt as if they were separated by an unruly sea. No, even now, the feet were more like inches. In her mind, Sybil knew Gideon's touch, his caress, and the warmth of his lips against hers. For so many months, she'd had no other option but to remember the way things had been—to hold them close during the long nights alone—after he disappeared, fearing she'd never set eyes on him again.

As of that morning, they were man and wife, joined in matrimony before all of London, witnessed by every person she held dear.

Nothing short of death would ever separate them—that was the promise Gideon had pledged to her.

Sybil was happy—loved, cherished, and lavished with affection.

When Gideon held his arms wide, Sybil didn't hesitate. She threw herself into his embrace.

"I love you, my dearest husband," she muttered, swallowing the sob that threatened to escape.

"I love you, too." Gideon pulled back, his intense stare searching her face. "Are you crying?"

"They are tears of utter joy, happiness, and love." Sybil moved back into his arms, pressing her cheek to his chest as she listened to the rhythmic beating of his heart, completely in tune with her own.

AUTHOR'S NOTES

Thank you for reading *The Lady Loves a Scandal!*

If you enjoyed *The Lady Loves a Scandal,* be sure to write
a brief review at any retailer.

I'd love to hear from you!
You can contact me at:
Christina@christinamcknight.com

Or write me at:
P.O. Box 1017
Patterson, CA 95363

www.ChristinaMcKnight.com
Check out my website for giveaways, book reviews, and
information on my upcoming projects,
or connect with me through social media at:
Twitter: @CMcKnightWriter
Facebook: www.facebook.com/christinamcknightwriter
Goodreads: www.goodreads.com/ChristinaMcKnight

Sign up for my newsletter here:
http://eepurl.com/VP1rP

Turn the page for an excerpt from
Bound by the Christmastide Moon,
featuring Sybil's brother Silas
and his love Mallory!

Ditchley Hall, Southampton, England
June 1811

SILAS ANSON, THE eighth Earl of Lichfield, glared across the vast, disorderly expanse of what he'd recently come to view as *his* desk, not the unfamiliar, cluttered stretch of flat surface that had once belonged to his father.

A man he barely remembered and could not conjure in his mind.

On the receiving end of Silas's scowl was none

other than Mr. Horace Peabody, Esquire.

The solicitor had also come with the Lichfield title and estate.

Though Silas silently debated which was of lesser value to him: his non-existent heritance or his father's trusted advisor.

"You are telling me—" Silas clamped his mouth shut, pondering and discarding his next statement as overly crass and unwarranted, no matter the validity of it. "You are telling me I was summoned back to England, ripped from my home in France, to inherit a title and estate so entrenched in debt that ruination can only be staved off for a month's time?"

Mr. Peabody, who surprisingly in no way resembled a pea of any sort, stared mutely at Silas from behind his rounded spectacles, his hands clenched on the stack of folders in his lap. Did the man realize how cliché he appeared? Glasses, ink-stained fingers, nerves so frazzled he shook, and the piles of paperwork. Lord above, the man had arrived with an entire forest's worth of the stuff. One could only imagine the mines exploited to collect the graphite needed to scribble all the nonsense that'd been presented to Silas.

And the solicitor had appeared anxious since his arrival.

"This plan you've so graciously detailed for me is the only viable option you have been able to ascertain for rescuing the Lichfield name?" Silas needed to hear Peabody verbalize his recommended course one last time; but the solicitor only nodded, his glasses slipping down the bridge of his nose. Silas wondered if he shouldn't seek other counsel in this matter—and every matter to come. "My estate is bankrupt, the title worthless, and my only recourse—if I refuse to throw myself at the mercy of my mother's family—is as outlined on this single sheet of paper?"

To further punctuate the absurdity of the situation,

Silas retrieved the aforementioned document with its hastily written paragraph and held it high for Peabody to inspect.

"That is, indeed, my recommendation, my lord," Peabody croaked, bowing his head.

If his father were not solidly in his grave, Silas would do away with the previous earl himself.

Bloody damnation, but Silas—along with his mother and siblings—had been content and otherwise entertained in Paris all these years. That was before he'd been unceremoniously summoned back to his father's homeland to usurp a title he'd never thought to possess.

Silas slumped in his seat and scrubbed his face, attempting to gain some clarity on the situation—yet, it eluded him still.

His mother, Mary Louisa Anson, Lady Lichfield, had absconded from England over fifteen years prior, her three young children in tow, never to see her husband again. Edmond Anson hadn't come looking for his family, hadn't sent so much as a messenger to check on their whereabouts or safety, nor the authorities to return his offspring to their rightful place in England.

As the years passed and no one came for them, Silas and his siblings adjusted to life in France as their mother pursued her passion for art. He'd assumed his father had forged a new life and continued as if his twin sons and young daughter had never existed.

The solicitor perked up, a new spark of hope lighting his otherwise lackluster stare. "You can always reach out to Mrs. Hambly. I have heard she is a fair woman who loves her relations. Do not so readily cast her—and your other aunts—aside. Perhaps the Countess of Somerton will be willing to step in and assist—"

Silas snorted. Yes, he'd been regaled with tales of the formidable Regina, his mother's sister, for years, and none of them spoke to her fair nature or love for her family, but rather to her need to be in control. "If my aunt cared a whit for her *relations,* she would have pursued my mother and offered assistance. Yet, my siblings and I lived on little more but stale bread and broth for years, residing above a butcher's shop in an unsavory part of Paris." Silas would not go into detail about the horrid conditions of his childhood—not with this man, at least. "No, that is not an option, at least not at this juncture."

"My plan will only solve a fraction of your problems, my lord." Peabody sighed, glancing toward the closed door of the study, his wide stare begging for any interruption as a means for escape. "And the solution itself is only temporary, at best."

"How could my father allow his estate to fall into such shambles?" Silas mused, expecting no answer, for any retort would not satisfy him.

"Because he was heartbro—" The solicitor's words cut short, and he swallowed. The tall clock chimed four times, echoing through the cavernous corridors of Ditchley Hall. "If there is nothing else you require, I will see myself out and prepare to depart for London."

Peabody stood, his lean, lanky body spoke of a man trapped behind a desk in a moldy room for over half his day, his pale skin in desperate need of sunlight.

Silas wanted the man gone, out of his office and away from Ditchley altogether. Away before word traveled to his siblings about the dire state of their affairs. Yet, that would not improve his family's situation nor hold the creditors at bay for long.

"Sit." His command reverberated off the walls and shook the windowpanes, sending a shiver down his spine. That was one positive of Ditchley Hall: his voice was a fearsome sound in every room. "I wish to speak further about my course for the next several months if I entertain your plan."

Regaining his seat, the solicitor shuffled through his folders in search of something, likely the means to keep Silas's wrath at bay a bit longer.

"An arranged marriage…"

"Yes, Lord Lichfield," Peabody nodded. "My notion to rescue the estate—at least for the time being—and keep your name and that of your siblings from the gossip mills, is to secure a mutually beneficial match."

"Mutually beneficial?" Silas had never envisioned himself wedded, especially after his parents' disastrous match. The only ones to suffer were the children of Edmond and Mary Louisa Anson. "What have I to offer a woman with a healthy enough dowry to sustain Ditchley Hall and provide for my siblings' immediate futures?"

Silas was speaking in questions once again, yet, when a man had no answers of consequence, all that was left was questions.

His entire life since fleeing England had been about finding answers…solutions to the many looming problems that plagued his family. When his mother had embraced her creative ways once across the Channel and neglected her children's upbringing, it had been up to Silas to find the means to educate his siblings, Slade and Sybil. He'd spent countless hours at the *Bibliothèque nationale de France,* first teaching himself to read, and then returning to their meager flat with the tomes necessary to instruct his brother and sister.

"You have a generations-old—and might I add, respected—title with connections to far more powerful members of society." Peabody recited the line as if he'd practiced it the entire journey from London. "That being said, I do not think it wise, or advantageous in your precarious position, to speak of the strained ties between you and your most notable relations."

Silas fairly growled. "Do you think me foolish enough to begin every conversation with the scandalous details of my mother's banishment?"

The solicitor's gaze swung back to Silas, his brow

furrowed. "Your mother—errr, Lady Lichfield—was not banished. Has never been spoken of in anything but the highest regard by my employer, I mean to say, the previous Lord Lichfield...your father." Peabody held up a single finger as he riffled through his papers once more. "Ah, yes, here it is. Your father commissioned this letter in the event that your mother returned to England after his death. It states that in accordance with British law, she is, always has been, and will remain, Lady Lichfield. While you are the Lichfield heir, your mother is entitled to a hefty allowance and an estate, if she so chooses to accept it."

Chooses to accept it.

Most peculiar phrasing, indeed.

"I'm assuming this has the stipulation that it is only enforceable after my father's death." The statement drew another uneasy glance from the solicitor, and bloody hell if Silas wasn't remorseful over his lack of enthusiasm to review the piles of paperwork littering his desk. "Because there is no other reason *my father* would have allowed his *family* to live in squalor in Paris if there were funds and property set aside for my mother."

The solicitor once again focused on the folder before him, flipping pages until he found what he searched for. He lowered his head further, his lips moving as he read. "There is no such clause, my lord."

"Then why—" Silas stopped himself once more, knowing his fury would find no peace by harming the messenger. There was little use demanding to understand the inner workings of his late father. "Let us return to your original plan."

"Very good, my lord." The man's head bobbed up and down, obviously aware he'd avoided Silas's displeasure for the time being. "I have it all written down before you."

"Yes, however, there seems to be one crucial flaw."

"Oh?" the solicitor asked, leaning forward over his

stack of papers to see the page on Silas's desk. "What would that be?"

Silas snatched the document and held it before him. "It details my need to wed—and marry for a healthy dowry—however, it does not purport *whom*, precisely, I should espouse." When the solicitor remained silent, he continued. "Being new to society, you should be well *aware* I am blissfully *unaware* of whom, exactly, has a sizeable dowry—and who will only bring increased hardship to the Lichfield name."

"I would never seek to command you in whom to wed, my lord."

Odd, as the man had sent numerous correspondences about what was needed to keep the earldom afloat for another quarter.

Silas massaged his temples as he eyed the solicitor.

Would anyone truly miss the incompetent man if he were not to make it back to London?

Yet, he must needs remember he was in England once more, not the uncivilized country of France—as most Englishmen were fond to classify those who chose to live across the Channel.

"By chance have you any *suggestions* for proper, financially well-endowed ladies I should seek to court?"

Peabody broke into a broad smile as if Silas had finally asked the exact question he'd been waiting to hear. "I happen to have a client who—"

"How very fortunate…"

"Yes, well, he is not actively seeking a marriage for his daughter but has sought my advice on several occasions in regards to finding a match for her."

"Her worth?"

"Pardon?" Peabody said with a gulp.

"What is her worth? If I am to sell myself to the highest bidder, I would know the reward is sufficient to see me through for several years." Silas would never entertain a union unless he reaped adequate benefits: funds enough to see his siblings accepted into society, and prestige to overshadow his mother's estranged family. "Also, I suppose I should hear what you know of the girl."

"Her dowry is sufficient if you adhere to my other advice on managing your estate and investing in appropriately modest ventures. The woman in question is the only daughter of a marquess—a wealthy and connected marquess. If you have aspirations for the House of Lords, he will be an admirable advocate."

"I have never seen myself as a political man."

"Then, perhaps, you will be more in line with her brother. He is an earl and quite the man about town. A confirmed rakehell with an untouchable reputation in business, and a propensity for the gaming tables."

This earl seemed more suited as a friend for Slade, as opposed to an ally for Silas. "I would have the family name."

"The Marquess and Marchioness of Blandford." The solicitor again searched his paper, his finger running down the page until he found what he sought. "Their daughter, aged eighteen summers, is Lady Mallory Hughes."

Silas only hoped the woman did not have a third eye—or worse, the facial hair of a man. Silas supposed the son of a flighty countess could not expect much on his return to England, and the advantages of the match certainly outweighed the negatives. He needed money and means to see him and his siblings settled among the *ton*. Things that his father hadn't seen fit to provide.

"You will handle the paperwork?" Silas inquired, his brow rising in challenge.

"Without a doubt, my lord." Peabody pushed to his feet again, clutching his folders to his narrow chest as the stack threatened to escape and cascade to the floor. "I will write him at once upon my return to London. I am certain he will entertain the match."

Silas remained seated as Peabody scurried from the

room. Odd a man of such height and thin frame could scurry, but that he did. With any luck, the solicitor would arrive in London and secure the proper paperwork within a fortnight.

The grandfather clock chimed once more—five loud gongs, echoing through the house, reminding Silas he was to meet his siblings in the grand hall for supper.

Coming soon in print, audiobook, and e-book!

ABOUT THE AUTHOR

USA TODAY Bestselling Author Christina McKnight writes emotional and intricate Regency Romance with strong women and maverick heroes.

Her books combine romance and mystery, exploring themes of redemption and forgiveness. When she's not writing, Christina enjoys trying new coffeehouses, visiting wine bars, traveling the world, and watching television.

Email: Christina@ChristinaMcKnight.com
Follow her on Twitter: @CMcKnightWriter
Keep up to date on her releases:
www.christinamcknight.com
Like Christina's FB Author page:
ChristinaMcKnightWriter